Alter Ego

Paul Daffinrud

ISBN: 1469961482
ISBN-13: 978-1469961484

Prologue

Last night he worked alone in the hanger removing the two front seats of the Cessna 152. The extra room in the cockpit was needed for other things. He would have to kneel during the flight, but he had trained himself for that and was confident the three-hour flight would not be a problem. The hard metal floor would be hard on his knees. _He must remember to bring a pillow._ When the seats were removed, he did a check of the plane and filled the gas tank. The small tricycle gear plane was ready.

The next morning he filed a false flight pattern with the girl at the office then drove his car to the hangar and parked as close as he could to the side entrance door. No one must see what he was carrying into the hangar. Satisfied he had everything, he put on the parachute. Below the parachute, he attached a canvas bag with survival gear and three hundred thousand dollars in cash. He opened the large door in front of him, got into the plane and taxied out of the hangar and onto the tarmac. It was going to be a good day for flying; there wasn't a cloud in the sky and the wind was blowing at five miles per hour. The entire state was experiencing the same weather; he couldn't have picked a better day.

His destination was Voyageurs National Park. The entire Park was forested but he had discovered an open field north of Lake Kapetogama on one of his trial runs. It was here that he would make his jump to freedom. The cops were too close; if he hadn't taken off today, he was sure he would have been arrested. He couldn't let that happen. Approaching the open field, he opened the side door, ready to jump. When the field came in sight, he turned off the engine and leapt out. The descent was perfect; pleased with how everything had gone so far he knew he would land in the center of the field as planned and then quickly disappear into the forested area. Picking up his chute and folding it, he noticed a ball of fire erupt several miles north of him. The ball of orange and yellow fire was soon followed by an ominous thick black cloud. The plane had crashed and it would be reported that he was in it. The search for him would finally end. He now had a fresh start, but he knew he would kill again

- 1 -

Sheriff Milo Bean reached in front of him and pressed the intercom button to the left of the bulletproof security door. As he waited for the door to unlock, he gazed at the watchful eye of the security camera aimed at the clear glass entrance door where he was standing. The dispatcher looked at the row of monitor screens directly above her head; a soft buzzing sound was emanating from screen number two. The black and white screen revealed an older man standing in front of the door, his silver colored hair cut short, almost too short, but it had been his trademark for the past thirty years. The dispatcher recognized Sheriff Bean and pressed the door release button. He entered and walked down the hall to his office. He had a dark brown parka draped over his left arm and his fuzzy winter cap with heavy earmuffs was held firmly in his right hand. It was Halloween evening and according to the reports on the radio and television, the weather was going to turn nasty. If the reports were true, and he had no reason to doubt otherwise, his deputies and the residents of Davis County were in for a long night.

Chief Deputy Frank Blume carried his full accoutrement of winter weather gear under his arm as he entered the Law Enforcement Center. He stood in front of the glass entrance door just as his boss had done a few minutes earlier. The lock clicked and he walked into the building. He immediately went to his office and carelessly flung the heavy clothing on one of the metal folding chairs that faced his desk; the clothes instantly slid off and lay in a pile of disarray on the floor. Frank looked down at the heap of clothes and decided to leave them where they were and checked the top of his desk for any messages. He was relieved to find there weren't any and went to the squad room to get a cup of coffee.

As he walked into the squad room, he noticed Deputy Crawford occupying one of two round tables in the small break room. He was perusing a crossword puzzle that lay on the table in front of him. The round table was enveloped with a dictionary, an atlas, a thesaurus, and a crossword puzzle dictionary. Frank poured himself a cup of coffee and glanced around the squad room. He appreciated the small room even though it had become much tinier over the years. When he first started on the department, it was four times its present size. As the department grew and more office space was needed the squad room had always been the obvious choice for the needed expansion for more space. The protests of the deputies were heard but never considered. They enjoyed the squad room and its dispensing machines for soda, candy, coffee, and sandwiches and didn't want to give them up; the break room afforded them some privacy when they took their breaks. One single-pot Bunn coffee maker now stood on top of a small wooden counter in the corner so as not to take up too much space and the machines were all gone now.

"How's the puzzle comin', Bones?" Frank asked, in a way that would suggest he was available to help.

"I'm stuck, I need a four-letter word beginning with 'L' and the clue is 'Lawyer's Exam'."

"Elsat," Frank answered.

"What?" Bones asked as he glanced up at him with an inquisitive look.

"Lsat," Frank answered, spelling the word. "It's the initials for the test lawyers have to take before they can get into law school. I took it a couple of years ago when I was thinking about bein' a prosecuting attorney."

Bones cautiously filled in the word. He didn't want to make any mistakes because he was doing the puzzle in ink as he always did. "It fits. Thanks, Frank."

Frank was more interested in what Bones was doing than he was in pouring his coffee and accidentally filled his cup too full. He sat down at the second table and gently placed the cup in front of him not wanting to spill any and not wanting to disturb Bones. He could obscure a whole table with his crossword paraphernalia and would not be a good conversationalist while he was working on it. Frank noticed a copy of the Bishop Gazette lying on the second table so he picked it up and scanned the four-page paper for any news of the approaching storm. There was none, only some local information regarding the birth of a baby girl, the death of a retired schoolteacher and some small town gossip.

"Heard anything about the storm?" Frank asked.

Without looking up from his puzzle deputy Crawford softly answered. "The latest report came in about an hour ago from the National Weather Service. The storm is supposed to start at about ten o'clock tonight and it's gonna be a doozie. The barometer's already starting to drop big time and the temperature's down ten degrees from an hour ago. It looks like we're gonna' get somewhere between ten and twelve inches of snow and high winds."

"Is the Sheriff here yet?" Frank asked.

"Yea, got here about a half hour ago, he's in his office."

"I think I'll go see him, catch ya' later." Frank got up from the table and refilled his coffee cup, with a little more caution this time, and walked out of the squad room and toward the Sheriff's office.

Frank tapped lightly with the knuckle of his index finger on the Sheriff's door and walked in. The Sheriff was sitting in his high back red leather swivel chair facing the wall behind him when Frank entered. Hearing the rapping on the door he turned his chair around to face Frank just as he was about to sit down. "Whatcha' thinkin' about Sheriff?"

"That damn Armistice Day storm. My father told me many horror stories about that day. It began with blue skies, warm temperatures and no wind. It looked like it was going to be a good day for fishing or hunting; the lakes and sloughs in the county were full of boats. The sportsmen thought this might be the last good day of fishing before winter set in. Within a few hours, the weather started turning ugly; the temperature dropped quickly and the sky darkened with storm like clouds. Soon there were blizzard conditions and many of the fishermen and hunters got stranded on the lakes. All in all thirty one people died that day."

Frank sat and looked at the Sheriff and tried to appear interested but he had heard the story at least a dozen times before. He wasn't as worried about the storm as the Sheriff was because every time one came along, the Sheriff was sure this was going to be worse than the Armistice Day storm. "Let's hope it's not."

The Sheriff got up from his chair and walked around to the front of his desk, leaned on it and looked at Frank. "I've contacted the Civil Defense and the rest of the deputies. They're all on standby for now but I don't think much is going to happen until early morning. The last I heard, the storm is going to begin around eleven and get worse throughout the night. Tomorrow we're gonna' have a full-fledged blizzard. Too early in the year for this shit. I've got Tom out in the county and he's radioed in a couple of times and everything is relatively quiet," the Sheriff said, with a concerned look on his face that Frank noticed right away. "I'm going home and get some sleep. I want you to stay here and if anything comes up, call me. Bones is here too and he can answer any calls that come in."

"Good idea," Frank answered, glad to see the Sheriff was taking care of himself. "Go home, get some sleep, and don't worry. There ain't no reason to worry, what's gonna' happen is gonna' happen. You can't control it. Everything here is in good hands and I'll call you if anything comes up."

At ten-thirty, Deputy Tom Jenks called in to the Sheriff's Department and reported a slight wind developing and a light mist in the air. "I can still make out most of stars but I can see some clouds moving in," the deputy reported. Other than Tom's call, the radio was quiet so Bones continued working on his puzzle while Frank stood in the dispatch area drinking coffee and talking to the dispatcher.

Frank Blume was promoted to Chief Deputy a year ago. He was second in command of the department and took his new responsibilities seriously. He had been with the department fifteen years and when the Chief Deputy decided to retire early Frank jumped at the opportunity to apply. He had the most seniority on the department and was the logical choice. Frank Blume became the new Chief Deputy of Davis County at the age of forty-one. He began his career as a road deputy and two years later was promoted to investigator and continued in that position until a year ago. Already in his early forties, his hair had become nearly as gray as his boss who was twenty years older. The thick mustache he had worn since he was in his twenties was now as gray as his hair. He understood the Sheriff's silver gray hair was the result of his worrisome habits but his hair was prematurely gray because of the lifestyle he had chosen and enjoyed. He drank too much coffee, inhaled too many cigarettes, downed too much beer, and did this all on a daily basis. Exercise was not a word that was in his vocabulary and he was at least thirty pounds overweight.

At five foot eight, his body had become disproportionately rotund; his chest, once robust had already sunk, his posterior completely covered any chair he sat on and his stomach sagged over his gun belt completely hiding the large brass buckle that held the weight of the leather and all its attachments together. He looked like he was nearing retirement age rather than his true age. His wife had nagged him for years to take better care of himself and he halfheartedly tried. When she divorced him two years ago, he got worse. With no one around to criticize his health habits anymore, he reverted to the life he led before he got married. But Chief Deputy Blume was a good man. He was honest as the day is long and his word was his bond. He was well liked by the other deputies and the people of Bishop.

At one-thirty in the morning, Deputy Jenks radioed the dispatch center informing them that the winds were increasing, the temperature was turning colder, and the mist he had reported earlier was turning to sleet.

At one-forty a.m., a 9-1-1 call came in to the dispatch center from Amy Garcia. She said her husband was threatening suicide. She was hysterical and crying as she tried to explain what was happening at the house. Frank was standing in dispatch, coffee cup in hand, when the call came in. He was familiar with the farmhouse and had been called there several times in the past couple of years. Luckily, the Garcia's lived less than a mile outside the Bishop City limits so the response time would be short. Frank didn't feel like leaving the building tonight, he wanted to stay near the radio center for updates on the storm. Reluctantly he went to the squad room and told Bones to get ready; they had been called to the Garcia farm.

"Of all nights for Bill to get drunk." Frank said as Bones backed the squad car out of the parking lot.

Frank knew it would be the same thing again this time. Garcia would be drunk. When he got drunk, he got depressed and when he got depressed, he wanted to kill himself. They would, as before, calm him down, bring him in, lock him up for the night, and have him evaluated by a psychiatrist from Cedarton in the morning. He would then be released until it happened again. Frank couldn't help think to himself that with the storm coming, Garcia might be in jail longer than he bargained for.

Frank and Bones entered the short driveway that led to the doublewide trailer the Garcia's were renting. They heard yelling coming from inside the trailer when they pulled up to the house. Mrs. Garcia opened the front door and began running toward the gravel township road. Bones hurriedly got out of the squad car and chased Amy Garcia until he caught her. He grabbed her, brought her back to Frank's squad, and sat her down in the back seat. Frank radioed Tom and asked him to come to the Garcia's for backup and then turned around and faced Amy Garcia who was in the back seat crying. "What's goin' on Mrs. Garcia?"

"Bill's drunk again, he's got one of our kitchen knives. He's sitting on the couch and has a knife pointed at his heart," she said, nervously looking out of the window of the squad and toward the house.

"I've got another deputy coming and when he gets here I'm gonna' have him stay with you. Deputy Crawford here and myself

10

are going to go into the house now, so just sit tight, Okay?" Frank said, trying to calm Mrs. Garcia. "You know, if we could just get your husband to stop drinking, we wouldn't have to come out here so much."

"I know, deputy, I've tried, I honestly have, the kids have tried, A.A. has been here, nothing works. He's really a wonderful man when he isn't drinking."

Frank noticed the headlights of Deputy Jenks car as it pulled into the driveway. Frank got out of the warm squad car, walked to the other squad, and told Tom that he wanted him to keep an eye on Mrs. Garcia while he and Bones went into the house.

Frank arrived at the front door first and was about to open it and enter when Bones yelled for him to get back. Frank did as he was told; Bones came closer and whispered that Garcia was standing next to the front door with a knife aimed at whoever came in the door.

"I saw his reflection in the hall mirror, he's behind the front door, and he has a knife." Bones said.

Bones and Frank drew their weapons and ordered Garcia out of the house. When he didn't come, the two deputies tried coaxing him out and when that didn't work, they knew they would have to enter the house and subdue him. Frank grabbed the front door knob and pushed it open slowly, keeping his eye fixated on the mirror and with his left hand motioned for Bones to follow. They were fortunate to have the hallway mirror to watch the movements of Garcia and to know his exact whereabouts. Frank quickly realized Garcia was not behind the front door anymore. He had lost sight of him. They entered cautiously and spotted Bill Garcia sitting on a weather beaten couch pointing a kitchen knife at his heart. Bones was able to distract Garcia while Frank quickly jumped him and easily forced the knife from his limp hand. He was so drunk that his hold on the knife was weak and it easily fell to the floor. Frank yanked him off the couch and handcuffed him and the two deputies escorted him out of the house and to the squad car. As Bones and Frank were driving back to the station with their prisoner they noticed the wind had picked up and the sleet was turning to snow. The roads were not yet icy but within an hour, if this kept up, the blacktop roads would be treacherous. Garcia was booked on a charge of attempted suicide and placed in a holding cell for the night. Bones and Frank went to the squad room and had a cup of coffee.

At five o'clock in the morning, the snow increased in intensity and the barometer was dropping fast. The National Weather service was recording winds of twenty-five miles per hour with gusts up to 40 miles per hour. The temperature had dropped to fifteen degrees and was threatening to drop further. Ice had formed everywhere; roads, trees, power poles, and telephone lines were all frozen.

It had been a long night for Deputy Jenks. The first traffic accident was reported at two-fifteen; it was a fender bender in the southeast corner of the county. He was twenty minutes away but no one was injured and they would just have to be patient until he got there. Six more accidents were reported during the night and he kept busy investigating them. The time went by fast and when Deputy Jenks looked at his watch again it was a little after five in the morning. He had been on duty since eight o'clock the night before but he wasn't tired. Three more accidents were simultaneously reported to dispatch within fifteen minutes of each other; they were reported from three different townships in three different parts of the County. He wouldn't be able to keep up so he radioed dispatch and asked for assistance. Overhearing Deputy Jenks radio traffic, Frank ordered Bones to grab a squad car and help Deputy Jenks. Deputy Crawford would answer calls in the southern part of the county and Tom would take care of the northern section.

At five thirty, Sheriff Bean entered the building and asked Frank to come to his office. "What's the latest on the weather, Frank?"

"Sounds like it's gonna' be a rough one; wouldn't be so bad but everything's all iced up. Same old story; first rain, then sleet, then snow. Makes for pretty bad conditions. I heard we got two inches of rain and sleet before the snow started."

"Yea, I heard the same thing. There's another eleven inches on the way and the winds are gonna' pick up. We better call in some more help; get me another half dozen deputies and the same amount of Civil Defense guys. We need more cars out in the county. We'll have them pair up and patrol the roads that are somewhat safe. I don't want to have to send a tow truck out to pull any of our squads out of the ditch. And we don't want them stuck in any whiteouts; they'd be worthless to us then."

Frank understood what the Sheriff meant by whiteouts. He had been caught in them before and it was a frightening and uncanny experience; the feeling of helplessness could easily overcome you and cause panic. Pulling to the side of the road and turning your overhead lights on was the only safe way to get through it. You were alone and the only thing to keep you company was your radio. The longest he was in a whiteout was four hours but most of them lasted less than that. Frank knew the dangers and would stress again to those going out into the county that if they got caught in a whiteout they were to pull as far off the road and turn on their overhead lights.

An hour after daybreak the six deputies and their Civil Defense riders were patrolling the county roads searching for stranded vehicles and assisting at accidents. By mid morning it was impossible to navigate the county roads so all help was called back to the office to wait out the storm.

- 2 -

Mary Helms sat at the kitchen table with her legs crossed and nervously crushed a cigarette out in a small tin ashtray. She was wearing a pink terry cloth bathrobe that was showing signs of wear and a matching pair of bedroom slippers. She opened a new pack of Kools that was sitting on the table, tapped the top of the pack on her index finger to settle the tobacco, pulled out another cigarette, and lit it. Satisfied that it wouldn't fall out of the ashtray she got up and poured herself another cup of coffee. Mary was on edge this morning and smoking too much. She watched her tenth cigarette of the morning burn down to the filter, snubbed it out, and turned her attention to her three children sitting at the table with her. They were quiet, occupied with eating their bologna sandwiches and sipping on chicken noodle soup. They didn't notice that their mother was troubled; she hid it well. Mary looked at each of the children. They were all older now and could take care of themselves if they had to. The weather reports were worrisome and she listened intently as the updates came over the radio. The farmhouse they were living in would not be good protection for them. There were so many cracks in the walls that the furnace couldn't keep up on cold nights. She heard the wind chill was going to drop to minus 100 degrees. She hoped the reports were wrong.

Janet was the oldest of her children and had turned twelve years old last week. Earlier Janet helped her mother gather the blankets and pillows that would be needed to keep warm and arranged them neatly on the floor next to the furnace. They would sleep in the living room tonight and cuddle next to each other for warmth. She hoped the furnace would stay working. Shara was ten and Tommy was two years younger. Shara appeared to grasp the seriousness of the situation but Tommy was too young to understand how grim their circumstances might become. Janet was mature for her age and instinctively helped her mother prepare for the emergency that seemed destined to come. Janet carefully prepared the temporary bedroom on the living room while her mother made a large kettle of soup. The soup would warm their little bodies and there was enough food to last them for at least five days; by that time, the storm would pass and the roads would be plowed.

Maybe she should have listened to her folks. They wanted her and the kids to come into town and spend the next few days with them until the storm had subsided and the county roads were open. She had always been a little stubborn and independent and didn't want to rely on her folks every time a minor crisis came along. This storm was not going to get the best of her. The four of them would do fine; she was hesitantly awaiting the challenge and knew that when the storm was over and they had survived, she would be proud of herself and the children. She had to admit to herself though that she would have liked Tom to have been here. She knew he had to work because of the storm but she would feel safer with presence.

"What's the matter, mother?" Janet asked. "You're so quiet."

"Nothing dear, just trying to think if I've got everything done before the storm hits."

Janet got up from the kitchen table and took her empty soup bowl and plate to the kitchen sink. She rinsed off her dishes and stacked them neatly on the kitchen counter. She poured herself a glass of water, took it back to the table, and sat down. "Where's Squeaky?" she said, looking around the kitchen for the dog. "He's always here when we eat, waiting for some food."

"That's right, Janet, where is Squeaky?" Mary asked, glancing at Tommy. "Did you let Squeaky outside again and forget to let him back in?"

Tommy dropped his head and looked at the floor. His voice subdued and muffled as he answered. "Yes."

Mary got up from the table, walked to the kitchen door, and opened it calling the dog's name. The dog immediately appeared and ran into the house, his tail wagging. Mary went to the stove, poured him a bowl of soup, and set it down next to his water. She sat back down at the table and watched Squeaky gulp down his warm meal. She thought of Tom as she watched the dog. He had brought it over one day as a gift to the family. He had found it as a stray and didn't have the heart to shoot it. The family fell in love with the dog immediately and it became a part of the family. She felt safe with Tom but realized that his job as a deputy sheriff would put a strain on their relationship. He loved his work so she put up with his crazy hours. Tom treated her with respect, not only as a woman but also as a person and she enjoyed that. Her ex-husband Ben was the opposite, he was the all-American macho husband who thought his wife should be his slave and she should answer to his every whim. Yes, she thought, if Tom asked her to marry him, she would.

Shara looked down and stared at her remaining soup. She was slowly stirring it with her spoon. "What do you think of Pastor Bartholomew?"

Mary curiously looked at her daughter. "Why do you ask that?"

"He looks like such a weasel to me," Shara answered.

"Shara," Mary answered, trying to look stern but secretly agreed that he did look a bit odd. "It's not nice to talk about people's looks. You should only judge someone by what kind of person they are."

"I know, mom, but I don't like him, I think he is strange. I mean when he was here today I thought he was looking at us awfully weird."

"I didn't notice anything weird about him dear. He stopped out just to make sure we were fine and would be okay if the storm hit. I thought that was very nice of him."

"Maybe," Shara answered as she finished the last of the soup in her bowl. She was acting nonchalant now as if the conversation was over and no one was going to agree with her. "I still think he is weird and his eyes remind me of the devil. I am not going to Sunday School anymore as long as he is there."

Mary was surprised at Shara's minor outburst. Shara always seemed to have more of an insight into things than the rest of the family did. Who knows, maybe Pastor Bartholomew was a little strange but he was harmless.

"Who was that other man that was here?" Tommy asked.

"I don't know Tommy," Mary answered, thinking that it was unusual to have two people stop by on the same day. Usually, no one ever came to the house except for Tom and her folks. "He said he was lost and looking for directions. I think his name was Diaz or something like that."

"He sure was asking a lot of questions, wasn't he, mom?" Janet asked.

"Yes he was, Janet. You know, for just wanting directions, he was asking an awful lot of questions." Mary answered, but now, thinking on it, she was curious as to why he wanted to know so much. She wondered why he was so inquisitive if anybody else had been there that day. She told him that her pastor was there and that ended the conversation and he left. Mary thought she better call Tom and tell him about their visitor. She called the Sheriff's department, asked for Tom, and was informed he was out on patrol and would not be in the office for quite some time.

Mary smoked one more cigarette, finished the last of the coffee, and then went into the living room to watch TV. Tommy and

Shara followed her while Janet stayed in the kitchen and washed and dried the dishes and tidied up the kitchen. Every fifteen minutes, the updated weather reports appeared on the screen. The storm looked like it might be bad but Mary felt prepared, comfortable and safe.

- 3 -

Frank had gone home to get some rest and when he returned to the office the storm had begun to subside. Feeling it was safe and being anxious to check the County, he decided to take his squad car and drive to Homer Township. It was the remotest area of the county and the farthest from Bishop. If there were to be any casualties from the storm or anyone in danger, it would be in Homer Township. Driving on county road 47 Frank was amazed at the amount of snow that was still on the roadway. He had thought the plows covered this area earlier but the winds must have blown the snow back onto the roads causing many drifts to accumulate. Frank was zigzagging back and forth with his squad car trying to avoid the newly formed snowdrifts. He felt like he was in an obstacle course like the one he had driven when he was at defensive driving school. Suddenly, a huge drift covered the complete width of the road. He stepped on his accelerator pedal with the full force of his right foot and hoped his speeding squad car would make it through the three-foot pile of snow. The drift was wider and deeper than he thought and he was stuck, all four of the tires buried and invisible, covered with snow that was over the wheel wells.

Frank radioed dispatch and asked them to send out a tow truck and impatiently waited for its arrival. He turned on the car radio for an update on the storm; he hadn't heard much of anything about the storm since last night. The Minneapolis radio stations did a better job of weather reporting so he fidgeted with the dial until he found the one he wanted. The Minneapolis station reported, "Davis County, along with Bishop and Cedarton, has been hit the hardest by the storm. Up until this time, there have been ten storm related deaths. The storm has now subsided but there are still occasional gusts of wind up to twenty-five miles an hour. The electricity and telephones lines are down in most of the area." The news of the deaths concerned him and he wondered if any of them were his friends or his relatives. He wished he would have stayed in the office and gotten the updates on the storm before leaving in his squad car. He would often get angry with himself because of his impetuousness; he would try to take things slower and think things through but was too set in his habits to change. The tow truck arrived a half-hour after his call, hooked up the thick cable to the rear axle of the squad car and slowly pulled the car out of the snow drift. He thanked the tow truck driver, got into his squad, and followed the tow truck into Bishop. He was not anxious to face the Sheriff; he was going to get his butt chewed and he deserved it.

He pulled into the station as the six deputies and Civil Defense workers were leaving to go home. The storm had abated and patrol duties were getting back to normal. Frank entered the Sheriff's department and walked to the Sheriff's office, gently knocked on his door and entered. He noticed that Bones and Tom were in the office and acknowledged their presence before he addressed the Sheriff.

"I suppose you know where I've been," Frank stated.

"Got stuck, huh, Frank," the Sheriff asked. "You shouldn't have gone out yet. The roads still aren't good."

"I know that now Sheriff." Frank answered, once again feeling stupid for his impulsiveness. "I was anxious to see what damage was caused by the storm. What have I missed?"

"Well," Deputy Crawford started. "I got about half of Bass Township checked before I had to come in off the roads. We got four deaths there and it looks like they got caught in the storm and froze to death. I got Mr. and Mrs. Sardonne, you know them; they live by the old Dunne creamery. Also, Don and Addie Jones, found them in their pickup. It had gone off the road and they got stuck and then ran out of gas; nothin' to keep 'em warm. The pickup was buried in several feet of snow when I discovered them."

"What about the Sardonne's?" Frank asked.

"I think they just got confused. You know they are both in their eighties. I found them outside their back door, huddled next to each other," Bones explained.

The Sheriff turned to Deputy Jenks, "Tell Frank what you've found."

"Three dead, Frank. It was the Benson family; I found them in the barn bundled under some piles of straw. They must have thought the barn would protect them or else they were worried about their cows. Anyway, they had a lot of broken windows in the barn and the wind just blew though so it was as cold in the barn as it was outside."

"That's only seven; I heard on the radio that there were ten deaths reported."

The Sheriff pulled out a list of all the dead so far and handed it to Frank. "The other three are on the list," the Sheriff said.

Frank looked at the list closely and was relieved to see that none of the names were friends or family or even anyone he knew. He handed the list back to the Sheriff. "I didn't get to any farmhouse. The driveways were so full of snow it would have been impossible to reach the homes. I found no stranded vehicles on the roads but couldn't cover much area because of the snowdrifts on. I wish I could have done more but it was impossible."

"What about the highway department, Sheriff?" Bones asked.

"I talked with the engineer and he has pulled off all of his trucks and graders until the wind stops. The weather bureau tells us the snow is over and visibility increased to a thousand feet. The winds are supposed to die by tomorrow morning so it looks like that is the earliest we can go out," the Sheriff answered.

The roads now plowed, the road deputies drove to their assigned township areas and checked farmhouses and road ditches for any casualties or anybody in distress. When the day was over, another eighteen bodies were discovered. Twenty-eight people had died in the storm. That night there was a candlelight vigil at the Abundant Life Church.

- 4 -

It was an oddity to witness sundogs in the early weeks of November. The phenomena occur on a cloudless day when the sun's rays refract off ice particles in the air. It has to be bitter cold for them to appear and the months of January and February are normally reserved for such a sight. On the third day after the storm, the temperature dropped to minus 20. The wind had calmed but the air remained heavy. It was as if the storm had tired the forces of nature and it was taking a rest.

The familiar orange trucks with their flashing blue lights were busy clearing the county roads. New power poles and telephone lines were being erected to replace the broken ones. Every home would have electricity within the week. Most driveways had been cleared; the farmers used their tractors with front-end loaders to remove the huge drifts of snow blocking them in and forcing them to be prisoners of their own homes. The Sheriff assigned Tom Jenks to patrol Brown Township; he was to stop at each farm and check on the welfare of the occupants and offer his assistance if needed. Tom had covered most of the township and found that everyone had survived the storm pretty well. By now, most of them were able to get into town and get the supplies they needed. Many of them stopped at the Bishop Cafe to have their first warm meal in three days.

Rookie Deputy Tom Jenks was the newest addition to the Davis County Sheriff's Department. He had joined the department less than a year ago and never regretted his decision. Prior to becoming a Deputy, he hadn't given much thought to what he wanted to do for a living or what path he wanted his life to take. He thought about this quite often and one morning he woke up from an exceptionally sound sleep and had an epiphany: he knew what he wanted to do with his life. He wanted to become a police officer. He couldn't explain how he came to make this decision but all his focus was now on directed to finding a job in law enforcement. A couple of weeks after his decision he noticed an ad in the Bishop Gazette. The Sheriff's department was advertising for a full time deputy sheriff. The Chief Deputy had retired and there was an opening for a road deputy. He applied, passed the written test easily, and was certain he would have no problems with the physical agility test. He had been a star football player for the Bishop Cardinals; he was lean, muscular, and overall in great physical shape. He had spent four years in the military police while serving in the Army. He placed first in the physical agility test and second on the written test. Although he had no college, the Sheriff recognized his time in the Army and accepted that experience in lieu of a college degree. He was hired from a field of twenty candidates and it was the most exciting day of his life. Tom Jenks was a hard worker and enthusiastic about his job; he easily gained the trust of the family of deputies that would be part of Sheriff Bean's force.

Mary Helms' two-story wood frame house was the last one on the list for Tom to check. He had kept her house for last on purpose. He was going to stop in and tell her he had the weekend off and would be spending it with her. As he drove down the township road toward Mary Jenks he remembered the night he first met her at the Duncan Ballroom. She loved to old-time dance and he did too; the polka, being their favorite, kept them on the dance floor most of the evening. Between dances, they talked and learned more about each other, their likes, their dislikes, their friends, high school, and Tom's life in the Army. Friends remarked at how well they looked as a couple and were sure that Mary Helms and Deputy Jenks would become an item in a very short time. He guardedly asked Mary if he could drive her home. She said 'no' because she had brought her own car. He did get a date with her in three weeks, his next weekend off. From that time forward, they were together every weekend.

Mary Helms lived her entire life in Bishop with her parents. Her father, Odell was the owner of the Graban Hardware Store in Bishop for as long as she could remember. Her mother, Betty, helped at the store if her husband was short handed. Other than that, Betty stayed home nurturing the care of their six children besides keeping the house clean and preparing the meals. Betty was adamant that "a wife's place was at home and with the children." With a dogged determination and a disregard for the modern view, she stuck to that belief. She enjoyed being a homemaker and a mother. Mary was the third oldest of the children and was thirty-two years old when she first danced with Tom Jenks.

Mary Graban grew up to be a pleasant, obedient, and somewhat docile child. She was her own best friend and preferred it that way. Mary was a conventional child and not different from the other girls her age. She was not overly attractive but not ugly either. Her grades throughout school were above average, getting mostly B's and C's. She did not get involved much in school activities and had no interest in music or sports. Her main love was reading romance novels, which she devoured at the rate of two a week.

The summer after she graduated from high school, Mary met Ben Helms. He was one year older than Mary and was employed full-time as an attendant at Jake's Texaco station. Jake's station was an old-fashioned small town gas station with six pumps. Ben would pump your gas, change your oil and filter, give your vehicle a lube job if needed or even wash your car if you asked him. Jake's was the only station in town; he enjoyed and prospered from having a monopoly. Ben was content at Jake's station and saw no need for an education. He quit school in the tenth grade when he turned sixteen. The next morning he reported for work at his uncle Jake's. Ben was not the ambitious type and was content with his life, desiring for nothing more than to work for his uncle the rest of his life. Ben owned a 1963 red Impala with black interior, a four-speed shift on the floor and 3 two-barrel carburetors under the hood. It would be hard to find any dust or dirt on Ben's Impala; when he wasn't tending pumps at the station, he was working and cleaning on his car in one of Jake's stalls. Ben Helms was aware of his good looks and kept himself well groomed at all times. He considered himself a ladies man and he was partly right. Mary was attracted to the young man that pumped her gas every other week. Ben flirted with Mary as he did with all the girls that came into the station. He had asked her several times for a date and eventually she gave in and said 'yes'.

Mary hadn't been on a date for over a year and was not sure if she would know how to act. She wasn't going to fuss over it though, Ben wasn't that special to her but she thought he was nice enough and that she might enjoy and evening with him. Their first date turned out to be very pleasant for Mary, something she wasn't expecting. Ben acted like the perfect gentleman and she felt safe with him. She was excited when Ben asked her for another date the following night; he suggested they take in a movie at Cedarton and she accepted his proposal. Soon they were dating on a regular basis and the relationship was turning serious. After a year of seeing each other on an almost daily basis Ben proposed and Mary excitedly accepted. The marriage ceremony took place at the Abundant Life Church and a luncheon followed. A wedding dance at the Duncan Ballroom concluded the festivities and the next day the couple was off to St. Paul for a short honeymoon. When they returned they moved into an old farmhouse that had been vacant for over a year. Mary's father owned the house and allowed them to live rent-free. After living in the house for a year, Ben Graban deeded the house and its three acres to the newly married couple.

Mary and Ben Helms discussed their plans for children on many occasions; both agreed they would like to have six, three boys, three girls. In the first six years of the marriage Mary had given birth to three children; they were half-way there. Janet, Shara, and Tommy were precious to Mary and she began to obsessively devote all her time to the children leaving very little time for her husband. With three children, the finances were getting tight. Even though they lived rent free, Ben didn't make enough money to support the family. He wanted Mary to work but she refused and wanted to stay home with the children just as her mother did. They began fighting frequently and they both sensed the marriage was deteriorating. Ben began flirting with he women that came into the station for gas and was soon staying out all night, with no explanation as to where he had been. Eventually Mary found out about Ben's several affairs and divorced him. The courts awarded her the house in the divorce settlement and ordered Ben to pay a meager child support. When the children started school Mary took a part-time job as a waitress in Bishop but money was always tight.

Tom pulled into the long, narrow dirt driveway that led to the farmhouse. It was a quarter of a mile long and full of deep ruts. There had been no maintenance on the driveway for years and Tom promised Mary that he would repair it this summer. When the spring thaws arrived, a four-wheel drive truck was the only vehicle able to maneuver its way to and from the house without getting stuck. As he neared the weather beaten, two-story farmhouse he realized for the first time what bad shape the house really was in and vowed he would help Mary fix up the place after he finished the driveway. The weathered gray wood was predominant over the original color of the house. Tom looked at the few spots of faded yellow that remained; the farmhouse was going to keep him busy this summer. The screen door was off its hinges and leaning against the entry to the back porch, the bottom frozen into the ground. The children's bicycles and wagons were still outside, half buried in the snow.

He parked his squad car and radioed the dispatcher his location. He walked to the house through unshoveled snow, onto the back porch where he noticed the back door was partially open and thought this was strange considering the weather. Maybe Odell and Betty had picked up Mary and the kids and forgot to close the door or it blew open. Tom pushed the door slightly and walked inside.

"Hello, anybody home? It's Tom."

There was no answer. Dead silence in the house; a silence that frightened him. He had a feeling something was terribly wrong. He slowly and quietly walked through the house, first the kitchen, then the downstairs living room and then finally to the bathroom and the pantry. He heard a soft whimpering sound coming from the upstairs and ran up the stairs taking them two at a time and yelling Mary's name. A docile Squeaky was waiting for him at the top of the steps and once Tom reached the second floor, Squeaky ran toward the upstairs bathroom, turning around a couple of times to make sure Tom was following. The bathroom door was half-ajar with Squeaky waiting in front of the door for him. Suspecting something was terribly wrong Tom carefully pushed the bathroom door open. From the tub area, he saw a little arm hanging out through the shower curtain. It was full of blood. He pulled the curtain back and his eyes fell on Shara, she was staring into nothingness; her throat slit. He could see she was dead. He paused to get a deep breath and to regain his senses before he went to Janet's bedroom. The door to her room was open and she was lying on her blood soaked bed; her throat slit in the same manner as Shara's. Tom rushed to Mary's bedroom, tears pouring down his cheeks. Panic and fear took over as he feebly yelled out Mary's name hoping for a response.

He found Mary lying on the floor by her bed. She was fully clothed and a large amount of blood was covering her dress; her throat slit like the others. He sat down next to her and held her dead body in his arms. As his senses slowly returned, he gently laid her down on the floor and ran outside of the house. He went to the squad, placed his hand on the fender, and vomited.

He was trying to think clearly but couldn't. He just stood there staring at the house when he remembered Tommy. He hadn't found him and had forgotten about him. He ran back into the house and searched the upstairs bedrooms again, trying to ignore the scenes in front of him. He found Tommy alive, under his bed. He was laying there on his back, staring at the bottom of the mattress above him; his thumb was in his mouth and his flesh was cold. Tommy had pulled a cover from his bed and wrapped it around himself to keep warm. He did not talk or acknowledge that the deputy was there. Tom gently pulled him from underneath the bed, held on to him tightly, and took him to the warm squad car and laid him down on the back seat.

Tom's hand was shaking as he grabbed the mike from its cradle and called dispatch.

"Come in, Tom," the dispatcher answered.

Tom tried to regain his composure as he started to relate to the dispatcher what he needed.

"I need the Sheriff to come to this location immediately. I'm gonna' need the coroner and I'm gonna' need an ambulance also. Have the Sheriff contact Josh Trimble and tell him I'm gonna' need the portable crime lab. You do know where I am?"

The dispatcher calmly answered the deputy that she knew his location and would make the necessary calls. "Are you going to stand by?"

"10-4"

It seemed like a long time to Deputy Jenks, but within twenty minutes, the Sheriff, the coroner and the ambulance appeared and slowly made their way up the driveway. The Sheriff's squad and the ambulance had their red lights on but no siren. Sheriff Bean pulled his squad car next to Tom's.

"What's going on, Tom?" the Sheriff asked.

"They're in the house, they've been murdered. All except for Tommy, he's in the back of the squad car. He looks like he's in shock; you better have one of the EMT's take a look at him, Sheriff."

Sheriff Bean went into the house to survey the crime scene and was in the upstairs bedroom when he noticed through the window the State crime lab pull into the yard. Agent Josh Trimble was close behind and parked his unmarked car next to the portable crime lab. Noticing the scene outside, he walked downstairs and out the rear door to meet Special Agent Trimble.

The two men shook hands and the Sheriff looked his friend in the eye. "It's pretty ugly in there, Josh; we got three murders, two of them are just little children and the third is the mother, Mary Helms. I'll let you guys go and do your job. My guys will stay out here and protect the crime scene. If you need anything, just holler."

"It's that bad, huh." Agent Trimble answered as he pulled out a camel cigarette from his jacket pocket and lit it. This might be his last smoke for a while and he wanted to enjoy it.

"Yeah it is. If you need any help from us let me know. I can pull Frank in to help if you like."

"Thanks, Milo. I probably will, but I'll know more after we get through with the crime scene."

- 5 -

Josh Trimble stood on the ice-covered porch and leaned on the wooden doorframe. Smoking a cigarette and studying his surroundings he was deep in thought. The Sheriff noticed his friend standing in the doorway and knew what was going through his mind; he was trying to piece together what had happened. Josh stepped carefully off the slippery porch and walked toward the Sheriff who was sitting in his squad car talking on the radio. The Sheriff rolled down his window as Josh approached. Josh leaned his elbow on the car door and asked the Sheriff if he would make contact with his Chief Deputy and have him come to the crime scene. "I think I am going to need Frank after all. The sooner he gets here, the better."

"He should be able to get here in about twenty minutes; I'll call him right away." The Sheriff answered as he picked up the mike on the dash and called his Chief Deputy.

Josh Trimble and Frank Blume had worked together on several cases in the past years and Josh had been more than satisfied with the job Frank had done, especially his willingness to do the follow-up investigations that were so vital in putting a case together. It was understood by the Sheriff that Agent Trimble would be in charge of the case and the Sheriff's department would assist

36

him and offer whatever help was needed. Josh was a Special Agent with the Minnesota State Bureau of Criminal Apprehension. His job was to handle the investigations of major cases for a County, if requested. The benefits to a county were enormous. The State had many more resources at their disposal, such as the crime lab, special investigative teams, along with the polygraph and handwriting experts. Individual counties could not afford these luxuries and were happy to have this type of arrangement with the State. The State was not interested in any type of publicity for itself and allowed the local Sheriff or Police Chief to take credit for the solving of a particular case.

"Go ahead," Frank answered.

"How soon can you get out here, Josh says he needs you."

"I can be there in less than a half hour. I heard what's going on out there and I've got everything I need in the squad."

"Good, I'll wait here until you arrive," the Sheriff answered, planning to leave and go back to the office as soon as Frank arrived. He knew that word of the murders had probably gotten out by now and he wanted to be in his office when the calls started coming in. Every radio station and TV station would be trying to contact him and every newspaper in the state would also be calling or were already at the Law Enforcement Center waiting for him.

"Frank's on his way out," the Sheriff said, hanging the microphone back on its metal clip as he looked up at Josh. "As soon as he gets here, I'm leaving. I'll be in my office if you need anything."

"Thanks Sheriff, I'm gonna' need twenty four-hour coverage out here. I can't have this crime scene disturbed. Have you got enough man power to do that?"

"It's going to cut me short, but I'll take care of it," the Sheriff answered.

Frank Blume pulled his squad car into the Helms driveway and pulled in front of the Sheriff's car. He got out and walked over to the Sheriff who was consoling his deputy, Tom Jenks. They talked for a few minutes and then Frank walked toward Josh Trimble.

"Haven't seen you for a while, where the hell ya' been?" Frank asked.

"I have been stuck in Burns County on a drug case, the damn thing is drawing out and should have been settled weeks ago," Josh replied. "It looks like the case is going to court next week so I am going to be busy and that's why I need your help."

"No problem, in fact, I was hoping you'd call me." Frank looked at the house, anxious to enter and look at the crime scene.

"The crime boys are inside now. They're dusting for prints, vacuuming and collecting blood and hair samples. When they're done inside we'll start our work," Josh said as he jotted some words down in his notebook.

"Do you need any pictures taken?" Frank asked.

"No, we've already got all the pictures we need. Videos too."

38

It was late in the afternoon and the sun was disappearing fast; Minnesota days were much shorter in the winter with maybe eight good hours of daylight. The crime techs patiently loaded their gear into the portable lab. They would return in the morning. The three bodies were loaded in the ambulance and taken to the hospital morgue. Tommy was transported to the local psychiatric unit of Bishop's small hospital. The sun was beginning its descent when Frank and Josh got into their cars to return to Bishop where they would meet the Sheriff. Deputy Blume radioed the dispatcher and had her inform the Sheriff they were done and would be in the office in about an hour. He informed the dispatcher that they would be stopping at the Bishop Cafe for a bite to eat before they came to the office.

The Sheriff was waiting anxiously, if not somewhat impatiently in his office when they arrived. Agent Trimble walked into the Sheriff's office first and Frank followed, closing the door behind him. Agent Trimble sat in the chair directly in front of the desk, pulled out a camel cigarette, his third of the day, and lit it. Josh pulled a yellow note pad from his briefcase and studied what he had written down at the crime scene.

"It was pretty nasty out there, never could understand someone killing an innocent little child." Josh stated, as he took a drag from his Camel. "How's Tom doing, Sheriff?"

"I think he's gonna' be fine. He's seeing a psychologist right now in Cedarton. It must have been a traumatic experience coming across those bodies the way he did. There was a rumor going around town that he and Mary were planning on getting married, but anyway, don't keep me in suspense any more, what'ya got?"

"As near as I can put it together, this is the way it went down. The killer entered through the back porch; entry must have been fairly easy because, first of all, the screen door was off and secondly the back door was unlocked. The lock didn't work and it looked like it had been broken for some time. I say killer, because I don't believe there was more than one. We found one set of shoe prints, that's all. The prints had traces of blood on them and were found in all of the upstairs bedrooms, the upstairs bathroom, the stairs, and the kitchen floor. If anybody else were involved, there would have been more than one set of shoe prints. The killer walked upstairs to Mary's bedroom, killed her while she was in bed, probably asleep. There might have been a little struggle and that would explain why she was out of the bed and on the floor. After she dies, the killer haphazardly cuts off her hair and tosses it on the floor beside her. My guess is that he used the same knife to cut off her hair as he did to slit her throat. It also looked like he pulled a ring off her finger. We found the ring on the kitchen floor. It's been bagged and on its way to our lab."

"This is interesting." Josh said as he scrutinized his notes. "On top of the dresser in the room where Mary was killed we found this card." Josh handed the card, now in a sealed plastic evidence bag, to the Sheriff. "What do you make of that?"

The Sheriff carefully examined the card, both front and back. He laid it on his desk, took off his reading glasses, and scratched his head. The card had been done in calligraphy and printed by hand; printed very neatly were six letters 'D.O.O.B.L.E.' Josh looked at the Sheriff "Beats the shit out of me what that means but I think it's our best clue."

"I've got two more calling cards here for you to look at, but let me continue. The killer then went to Janet's room and killed her while she was sleeping. There was no sign of a struggle and I'm guessing she died instantly. He then cut off her hair as if this was some kind of ritual for him and tossed the hair on the floor." Josh handed another card to the Sheriff and placed it on his desk next to the first card. The second card, also done in calligraphy, read 'DEATH. O.O.B.L.E.' "That card was found on the dresser in Janet's room. It was stuck in the corner of the mirror where there was a space between the mirror and the mirror frame."

"The killer now entered Shara's room. By this time she must have woke up and was screaming or something. We'll have to wait for the pathologist's report, but my guess is he swung the knife at her but only nicked her. There was blood in the bed so he must have caused some bleeding. She was probably still screaming so he grabbed her and took her into the bathroom, dumped her in the bathtub, and killed her there. I think the murder happened in the bathroom because her hair was cut off in the tub and left there. Also, there was another card in the bathroom, lying on the bathroom vanity."

Josh placed the third card on the desk next to the first two. The Sheriff looked at it in confusion. This one read 'DEATH. ON. O.B.L.E.'

"What we got here, some kind of a psycho?" the Sheriff questioned. "I mean, this guy had these cards printed before he even went to the house. There's your premeditation, Josh."

"You bet," Josh answered. "The sequence of the cards tells us the order of the killings also. He even had that planned. The placement of the cards and the bloodied shoe prints pretty much give us a clear picture of what happened."

"Can you place a time of death?" the Sheriff asked.

"We don't know, the coroner hasn't done his report yet but I am guessing it was the early morning hours of the day Tom checked the place. The County had plowed the road the afternoon of the day before; prior to that it would have been impassable so we know with some degree of certainty the murders took place after the road was open. Tom said the bodies were still warm and rigor mortis had not yet set in. The temperature in the house was eighty-two degrees and the furnace was working to full capacity. My guess is they hadn't been dead for more than five or six hours."

"What do we do now, Josh?" the Sheriff asked.

"We can't do much until we get all the reports from the lab and the pathologist."

"Anything else I should know before I talk to the press?" the Sheriff asked, trying to figure out how he was going to present this to the news media without causing alarm in the community.

"A couple of more things are all. First of all, we think the killer knew the family. He seemed to know where everyone slept and the layout of the house. There didn't appear to be anything ransacked so burglary was probably not a motive."

"That means our killer lives in the area or did live in the area at one time," the Sheriff stated.

"More than likely, but not definite," Josh answered. "I mean it could have been somebody who just stopped in for some reason and cased the house out. It could have been someone posing as an insurance agent, wanting to get dimensions of the house. I mean, who knows at this time. But, I am leaning to someone more local than not."

"What about a profile?" the Sheriff asked.

"I'm meeting with our psychiatrist tomorrow to give him what we've got so far. By that time, we'll have the pathology report. He'll want to know if there was any sexual molestation committed on any of the victims. The patterns that have been developed by the killer, the hair being cut off, the manner of death and the ring taken off should be a big help in putting together some kind of profile. If there's nothing else, Sheriff, I'm going for a beer."

"Just one last thing I'm curious about. Tommy. Why wasn't he killed too?"

"Don't know. Maybe he was just after the girls. Maybe he overlooked Tommy, forgot about him, or didn't even know he was there. It was just lucky he hid under the bed."

"You guys have had a long day," the Sheriff said, acknowledging Frank and then Josh. "Have a beer for me too."

- 6 -

Special Agent Josh Trimble was forty-eight years old but looked much younger. His self-discipline, confident approach to life and assiduous work ethic were learned behavior while serving in the Marines. His sandy blond hair was without gray, cut military style and worn that way since the Marine Corps barber cut it for the first time. His tanned skin was a self-creation, the result of a tanning booth at the shop of his hair stylist, which he visited faithfully every three weeks. Along with his six-foot two-inch body, he had developed a solid frame of one hundred ninety pounds. He purchased a flexi-gym six months ago and worked out on it faithfully most nights. He had weaknesses, smoking and drinking were the worst. He was determined to quit the cigarettes but didn't think he would ever stop drinking beer.

He was more conscious of his appearance now that he had divorced Marilyn. After twenty-four years of a failed marriage, he enjoyed being single again. The bitterly contested divorce took over a year to settle in the courts. It was the best thing he had ever done and was happier now than he had been for years. Their married life had been a failure from the start and he wondered what he was thinking when he asked her to marry him. He and Marilyn were two different people but he didn't realize it until a couple of years into the marriage. Things got progressively worse the longer they were together. Josh reached a point where he couldn't handle it anymore and finally asked for a divorce. He was the happiest he had been since the Marines.

Special Agent Josh Trimble had been in law enforcement for the past twenty years. He began his career as a beat cop in Bishop. At that time, it was a small two-man department with one squad car and a small office in back of city hall. The town of Bishop was a bedroom community and still was. He and the Chief covered the town 24/7 with a little help from the Davis County Sheriff's Department. There were few calls in those early years and he and the Chief easily handled them. He was the only one who applied for the job and hired on the spot. The Police Chief was thankful that someone even applied. The pay was terrible and the hours were horrendous, Josh knew that going in but was confidant a good career lay ahead of him, he felt it in his bones. He was a patrol officer in Bishop for five years and during that time managed to get his bachelor's degree from the nearby college in Cedarton. After graduating from college and still working in the City of Bishop, Sheriff Bean offered him a job as one of his deputies. The County was growing and the County Board had authorized the Sheriff to add one more deputy to the department. The Sheriff had liked Josh and offered him the job. He was with the Sheriff's department for six years when an opening came up with the State Bureau of Criminal Apprehension. He applied and got the job. It was his military background, his law enforcement experience and his bachelor's degree that interested the Bureau and they were happy to offer him the job. With several years experience on the bureau, he had become one of their best agents.

The years in law enforcement, for the most part, had been good to him. Sometimes his mental attitude soured with the sordid side of life but he adjusted and loved his work. At times, he got tired of dealing with the jerks of the world and thought how nice it would be to have a nine-to-five job, come home to the family, leave the job behind him and enjoy the evening with the kids and the wife. These thoughts didn't stay with him long though and he would tell his friends that he came to his senses after a few seconds of thinking about this. That kind of life wasn't for him.

He pulled his dark maroon Minnesota State unmarked squad car into the parking lot of Pete's Tavern. It was his favorite hangout and it was where the other cops hung out. They served his favorite beer on tap and in a frosted mug, the only way he liked it. He walked in, picked a stool at the bar, and ordered a beer. The small tavern was quiet except for Pete and two other patrons he didn't know.

"Here ya go," Pete said as he handed the frosted mug of beer to Josh. "Been a rough day, huh?"

Josh looked at Pete; he admired the man for what he had made of himself. It was nineteen years ago that he arrested Pete for DWI and he hadn't had a drink since. He was the meanest, drunkenness and fightingest man that Josh had ever encountered. He was drunk every night in those days but when he was sober, he was a quiet and peaceful man. With Pete, the alcohol created a Dr.

Jekyll and Mr. Hyde personality. He was now a successful businessman and owned a lot of property in and around Bishop.

"Sure has. Where's everybody tonight?" Josh answered.

"They are all scared shitless, my friend. After what happened today, no one's going out."

"I can sure as hell understand that. It's a tragedy all right. What's the word around town?" Josh asked hoping to pick up some of the local gossip.

"Everybody seems to think her ex did it. He's the only one with a motive. What do you think, Josh?"

"Don't know yet. I'm heading to St. Paul tomorrow to get the lab results. Maybe we'll know more then." He ordered his second beer, drank it slowly, and went home to bed.

When Josh left the next morning, he noticed the exceptionally brilliant orange of the sun as it began its rise. The sky was clear with a slight trace of the sundogs that had been appearing lately. He never paid much attention to the beauty of nature but this day it caught his attention. He pulled out of Bishop and onto Interstate 35 and drove north to St. Paul. He stopped at Cedarton for breakfast and a quick glance at the paper. He wanted to read what the media had to say about the murders. He could tell, after reading the story, that Sheriff Bean hadn't released much information. That was good. He looked at his watch and decided it was now time to get back on the road. He didn't want to get to the office too early. He wanted the lab boys and the pathology reports to be ready for him when he arrived.

He pulled into the bureau parking lot at nine-ten; he had allowed an hour for the reports to be done and sitting on his desk. He would read them and if he had any questions, he could contact the lab boys later.

He entered the building through the back door, walked to the coffee room, and said his casual good mornings to the coffee drinkers and donut eaters. He poured a cup and went directly to his office. The reports were on his desk, neatly piled and separated into categories of evidence. He went through them slowly, carefully, and methodically. He didn't want to miss a thing. He was going to bring the reports back with him but wanted to run them through his mind while driving back. He pulled a lined, yellow legal pad from the top drawer of his desk and jotted down the highlights of the reports.

Time of death: Approximately 0200 hours on November 3.

Cause of death: Severed carotid artery, death was instantaneous. All three victims died in the same manner. Weapon used was more than likely a large knife, possibly a hunting knife.

Sexual improprieties: None of the victims had been sexually molested in any way. Semen tests were negative on the body cavities of the victims.

Blood samples: All blood samples taken at the scene were found to be those of the victims. No other blood type found in the house. The blood samples left by the shoe prints had traces of blood from all three victims.

Fingerprints: None found other than those of the victims and those investigating the crime scene.

Shoe prints: Only one pair of shoe prints were found indicating that the killer acted alone. Lab reports showed the prints were made by well-worn tennis shoes or possible some type of sneaker. One set of prints, origin unknown, found on the back porch.

Calling cards: Type of ink used and type of paper used are contained in the report. (follow up needed on this to determine where it may have been purchased.)

Tire tracks: None due to inclement weather conditions.

Other evidence: None.

Killer profile highlights: Difficult to put together much right now. Killer was more than likely a severely abused child. He may have homosexual tendencies due to the fact that he did not sexually molest the victims or he may have a hatred for women because he had been a failure with them. He may be a religious zealot due to the ritualistic way the victims were murdered. Satanic sacrifice is also a possibility here also, though Satan worshipers usually carry out their violence as a group and not individually. The hair being cut off could relate to something biblical. (Too many possibilities here, would like to gather more information if possible to pinpoint more detailed and specific profiles.)

Satisfied he wrote down the information he needed, he went to the copy machine and printed several copies of the reports to take back to Bishop.

When he arrived at his office in Bishop, he asked the dispatcher to contact the Sheriff and tell him he was back and he had the information the Sheriff wanted. He was informed by the dispatcher the Sheriff was out for the day and that he would not be back until tomorrow afternoon. He took a copy of the reports and placed them in a large manila envelope marked PERSONAL AND CONFIDENTIAL and put it on the Sheriff's mail cubicle in the secretary's office.

It was mid-afternoon and Josh decided to call it a day.

- 7 -

The one story brick building erected in 1928 was the last one constructed on Main Street for several years. It was built to accommodate a men's clothing store, but the Great Depression that occurred a few years later forced the small clothing store out of business. The building remained vacant until the end of World War II when a returning sailor decided to follow his dream by turning the vacant building into a restaurant. He aptly named it the Bishop Cafe and it was just as popular in the small town today as it was when it first opened. It was two months ago that Bill Johnson applied two coats of white paint and a sporty dark green trim on the outside façade in return for a month of free breakfasts. The customers remarked on what a wonderful job Bill had done and how nice the outside of the restaurant looked. The makeover was the first one in six years and the owner felt it was time and couldn't beat the bargain she had made with one of her favorite morning customers. The old façade, painted a rather sickening green, was weathered and the white trim that was supposed to compliment the main color was non-existent, worn away from years of harsh weather. The Bishop Cafe's new color was the talk of the town and it met with favorable revues from everyone. Several owners had come and gone through the years and now Dolly Peters was the latest owner. She had owned the Bishop Cafe for the last five years.

Every morning at 6:30, Dolly unlocked the front door and welcomed her first customers of the day. Day after day, week after week, month after month, and year after year the same faces walked through the single glass door anxious for their first cup of coffee. Some awake and alert, others not quite so lucky, they meandered to their favorite table, table number two and sat down, ready to talk politics or business or just wake up. Most of the early morning crowd were local businessmen. Most of those at the table ordered coffee only; Dolly made no money off them in the morning but many of them came in for lunch and spent generously. The customers at table two sat in the same chairs as they had the previous day, more out of habit than anything else. Some came in happy at that early hour of the morning, while others were languid, forced to face another day but they all left in a better mood than when they came in. It was a jovial group, discussing mostly politics, local and national. Most were in agreement and most were Republicans.

Bill Johnson sat at the end of table two and read the Bishop Gazette while still listening to the conversation going on around him. He was the recognized local handyman around town and could fix anything from a leaky faucet to a broken air conditioner. Tall and thin, his hair had whitened over the years. Bill Johnson would soon be sixty-five and receive his first social security check. He thought that he would slow down after that first check came in the mail. He was a simple man and wore a simple wardrobe, blue jeans, a blue denim shirt, and a green John Deere cap; his attire for as long as anyone could remember. Bill Johnson was a self proclaimed atheist and socialist but worst of all, especially at table two, he was a

Democrat. He loved to argue and sometimes the conversations at table two got very heated.

Clem Scott sat to the right of Bill and many times the two men would quietly discuss things with each other and ignore the rest of the table. Clem's silver gray hair and mustache distinguished him as the oldest member of the group. He kept Bill supplied in caps.

Nick Jones was the wealthiest and the youngest of the group. He was an insurance agent and his company held policies on almost everyone in Bishop. His neat appearance, businesslike attire and slight arrogance of demeanor left no doubt in one's mind that he was, at the least, somewhat successful.

Kevin Arnold sat across from Nick Jones and kept to himself most of the time. Employed by the local telephone company he worked as a lineman. He didn't fit into the group but faithfully showed up every morning. He enjoyed the conversations taking place around the table and considered his time at the Bishop Cafe the best part of his day. He eagerly consumed every word that was said at the table and then went to work and passed his new found knowledge and gossip on to his fellow workers.

Barry Anderson and Andy Didier were also part of the early morning faithful. They owned A & D Chevrolet and kept everyone informed about any new used car that came in and what a deal they could give on it. They were also Republicans and were delighted when the table ganged up on Bill Johnson.

Clem looked over and noticed Bill had finished his paper, folded it and set it down in front of him. "Whatcha' think about them Helms murders?" Clem asked, breaking the silence at the table.

"We all gotta die sometime," Bill stated.

"'Cept you. You're too ornery to die," Andy Didier popped in.

"Let's face it. Even I gotta die. Last night, though, I was thinkin' that if I got real sick, you know, where I thought I was going to die, that I don't want to be put on no life support shit. I decided right there last night what I'm gonna' do, if I get that bad. I'm gonna buy me an airplane ticket to Chicago. When I get there, I am going to find me a Mafia guy and go kick him in the shins as hard as I can, then I am gonna' just stand back and wait for him to shoot me."

Barry Anderson laughed with the rest of the group but wanted to get more serious, "My wife is really scared. She's afraid to even go out of the house until they catch this guy."

"I know what you mean," Andy added. "We're worse off. We live in the country and there are no houses near us to get help if we needed it. My wife wants me to take her and the kids and move in with her folks at Cedarton until this is over."

"Has anybody heard anything other than what's been in the paper?" Clem asked.

"As far as I know, the sheriff's department has no clues whatsoever," Nick added just before taking a sip of his coffee. "You'd think with the tragedy they had out there they'd find something," Nick finished, putting his empty cup back on the table.

"I think they know who did it, but jest ain't telling us yet. I think it was the ex, you know, Ben Helms. They say he was in debt up to his ears and if Mary and the kids were out of the way, he wouldn't get stuck with those child support payments."

"I hear he had insurance on the whole family. Ain't that right Nick?" Andy asked, expecting Nick to volunteer the right answer.

"You know I can't tell you that, Andy," Nick answered him sarcastically.

Clem noticed the front door of the cafe open and looked up to see who was entering. Everyone that came through door was scrutinized by the entire group at table two, except for Bill. Satisfied the customer who entered was familiar they continued with their discourse of the morning. Clem nudged Bill, motioning him to look toward the door. "Good morning, Josh," Clem almost yelled, trying to get his attention.

"Mornin' Clem," Josh said, acknowledging everyone else at the table also.

"Why don't you join us," Clem asked in a slightly persistent way.

"All right," Josh replied, not wanting to be rude. He had planned on grabbing a booth and eating alone. He preferred that in the morning so he could read the paper without being bothered.

"We want to know what's goin' on with these Helms murders you're working on," Clem boldly asked, being the busybody of the group.

Josh didn't want to talk about the subject and especially to this group. He noticed he had the full attention of the table so he gave them a brief account of what happened and hoped they would drop the subject.

"Got any suspects?" Clem asked, not letting up on the subject.

"No."

"Do you think he was local?"

"We can't assume anything at this point," Josh answered.

"What about Ben Helms?" Andy asked.

"He's not a suspect at this time. Do you think he did it, Andy?"

"Don't know, just asking is all."

Dolly, noticing that Josh hadn't been waited on quickly poured him a cup of coffee and a glass of water and brought it to the table. "Anything else for you this morning, Josh?"

"Yea, give me the special over easy," Josh answered after looking up and noticing what was written on the chalkboard informing him of the special of the day. "Looks like you are really busy this morning. What'd ya do, tell everyone you were going topless this morning?"

"No," she answered with a smile. "The weather's finally turned warmer and everybody's gettin' out of the house," she said as she slapped a menu on the top of his head.

Josh laughed. He had known Dolly ever since she started working at the Bishop Cafe years ago. She had been frugal with her tips and when the previous owners decided to sell the restaurant, she bought it, paying cash. She and Josh were the same age and he had even thought of asking her to go out with him, but he hadn't got around to it yet. She worked fourteen hours a day, seven days a week, which didn't leave much time for dating. She had always been a workaholic and it is no wonder she never got married, Josh thought to himself.

While Dolly was writing down Josh's order, the front door opened and the table's occupants looked up and noticed Pastor Bartholomew enter. He grabbed a chair from another table and slid it over to table two where he positioned himself to the left of Bill Johnson. Pastor Bartholomew was the newest member of the group seated at the table. He was pastor of the largest congregation in town and some say, the only 'real' congregation in Bishop. The Abundant Life Church hired their new pastor six months ago but it was only within the last two months that the pastor discovered the Bishop Cafe and its morning coffee clutch. He was there every morning except Sundays and Wednesdays. Wednesdays were his day off.

"When's the funeral?" Clem asked.

"Hasn't been set yet Clem," the pastor replied. "The obituary isn't even done yet. You know, they were a really nice family but were going through some hard times lately."

Except for Bill and Josh, the ears of the group focused in the direction of the pastor. He continued, "they didn't come to church much, but once in a while Mary would drive the kids into town and bring them to Sunday School. I think I've only seen Mary in church once since I became pastor. A couple of times I brought some clothes out for her and the kids that were donated by members of the church. I've also taken food out to them every once in a while and I know they were appreciative of it. Mary and the kids also got support from her parents so I think they were able to survive, but just barely. That reminds me, you guys could donate some food to the church's Food Shelf; we're kind of getting low. Anyway, I really felt sorry for them. I know Ben wasn't making his child support payments and the money she was earning hardly covered their basic needs."

The pastor finished and turned to Josh and unexpectedly stated. "I think Ben's your man."

Josh looked at the pastor, shrugged his shoulders, and decided it was time to leave. He had finished his breakfast so he took a couple more quick sips of coffee and got up and left.

- 8 -

Losing a daughter and two grandchildren transformed the dark auburn hair of Betty Graban to foggy gray. The stout, hard working woman metamorphosed overnight into a worn out and thinning woman; she barely ate enough food to sustain herself. The ever-present sparkle in her eyes had dulled to a sad, sardonic blue. Betty Graban, mother, grandmother, homemaker, churchgoer, and community leader had suffered a loss that her strength could not bear. Odell Graban, the tall, solid, and stoic man who had always been so sure of himself became lethargic. No longer did he play his childish pranks on his family and friends. His smile vanished, his enthusiasm for work and life died; his optimism turned into ugly pessimism. As time, in its slow and patient way, went on, the wounds suffered would eventually disappear and life would somehow get back to normal.

Betty had always been the weaker of the two and was trying to keep herself busy by contacting relatives and making the funeral arrangements. She wanted it all over with but knew the funeral would be postponed for a couple of days so the relatives of the family could get to Bishop to attend. She also knew there were going to be autopsies and lab tests connected with the investigation.

She resigned herself to the fact that the funeral would not take place as soon as she would have liked. Many of the townspeople came to the house to offer condolences, bringing with them baked goods, salads, hot dishes and candies to help with the food that would be needed in the next few days.

Odell and Betty had lived in the large white two story wooden frame house all their married life. Odell had been born in the house and grew up in it. Odell never left Bishop like most of his classmates had done; he graduated from Bishop High School and immediately went to work for Davis Hardware. He worked for Mr. Davis until he retired and bought the store from him. Odell was walking through the store one last time before he would close it temporarily. The thoughts of the crime were racing through his mind. He was trying to piece the puzzle together but it was as if there were no pieces to start with. He had the oddest feeling that the killer was from the area and had known Mary and the kids. None of the other clues were of any help to him now but maybe, just maybe, they would mean something later. He would have to meet with Josh Trimble and Deputy Blume after the funeral and hoped he would be mentally up to the task of reliving the murders over again.

The beautiful autumn weather had finally begun. Indian summer, so cherished by the Midwesterners arrived with a great and sudden splendor. The farmers were once again in their fields harvesting the remaining corn and soybeans. The leaves had fallen from the trees and onto the yards creating a collage of burnt orange, brown, yellow, and red colors. The trees, except for the evergreens, were now dormant, stripped of their leaves and left bare for the long winter ahead.

The funeral was held in the second week in November, one week after the slayings. The Graban family met at the house before going to the church. Tommy had been living with them since the deaths of his mother and sisters. Squeaky had come with Tommy and the two of them became inseparable, as if sharing a strange, secret common bond.

Tommy had not spoken a word or uttered a sound since the murders. No manner of coaxing from his grandparents or friends would help and he had become as if a deaf mute. He was meeting with a psychiatrist on a daily basis and was diagnosed as having a form of post traumatic syndrome. The psychiatrist could not be reassuring to the Grabans, explaining that this condition could last for weeks, months, and even years. Tommy could not be taken to the church, so the neighbor girl, Cheryl Baker, came over to watch Tommy and Squeaky while the family attended the funeral. Cheryl seemed to be the only person Tommy wouldn't run away from if she tried to talk to him. Betty hoped Cheryl could handle Tommy but knew she would have to take her chances on this day.

The Abundant Life Church, filled to capacity with friends, family and the curious quietly waited for the service to begin. Folding chairs were set up in the hallway; the social hall was equipped with loudspeakers for the overflow. The local cable company from Cedarton filmed the funeral for broadcast on their local channel. It was the largest funeral in Bishop that anyone could remember.

Tom Jenks, in a marked squad car, led the funeral procession through town and up Main Street to the Bishop Memorial Cemetery. Tom's red overhead lights were engaged and he kept the procession at fifteen miles per hour. The town would remember this funeral for years to come he thought to himself. Driving and thinking he still could not make any sense out of the killings. What could possibly be a motive? Mary and her family had never harmed anyone. They were peace loving and good people. The whole thing was crazy. He wished he had more experience in investigation and maybe some clue, some small piece of evidence that would put it all together. He hoped Agent Trimble would eventually solve the case but how long would it take and who was this monster that was still out there. Did he live in Bishop or Cedarton or the Twin Cities or was he a drifter travelling through? He wondered how he would feel once the killer was caught. He hated the man and wished the State had the death penalty; the killer certainly deserved it. Were these feelings a cop should have? His mind returned the job at hand as he pulled into the cemetery with the hearse following behind. The funeral procession was long as over a hundred cars entered the cemetery behind the hearse. He would stay for the burial service and drive back to the church for refreshments at the social hall. He wanted another chance to offer his sympathies to the family.

It had been a long and exhausting day for Betty and Odell and they arrived home much later than planned. They both felt relieved when the ordeal was over. They walked into the house and noticed Cheryl sitting at the dining room table and they could see she had been crying. Odell hung up his coat in the closet and looked at Cheryl and then at the television in the living room; two large cracks in the screen caught his attention. He stared at the television for a while and then turned to Cheryl.

"What happened to the TV, Cheryl?"

"Tommy did it, Mr. Graban. Please don't get mad at him. He's up in his room and won't come out," Cheryl answered, as she wiped her eyes with a tissue. "We had the funeral on the TV when both Tommy and Squeaky went crazy. Squeaky starting barking and barking and then running around in circles. He barked the whole time the funeral was on. I couldn't shut him up. I tried to catch him but I couldn't. I wanted to lock him downstairs because I couldn't stand the barking but I couldn't get a hold of him. He's upstairs now with Tommy."

"That's very strange, Cheryl, but what about the TV?" Betty curiously asked, staring at Odell and then at the TV.

"Tommy threw your iron at it, Mrs. Graban. He threw it as hard as he could and it would just bounce off. He kept picking it up and throwing it until it finally broke. I couldn't control him. I tried grabbing him but he would get away. I yelled at him too and he wouldn't listen. It was like I wasn't even here. It broke just as the pallbearers were wheeling out the caskets. After it broke, he went up to his room and wouldn't come out," Cheryl said, trying to control her sobbing as she told the story.

"Was Tommy crying?" Betty asked and began shaking uncontrollably as her husband held her and tired to comfort her.

"No, there were no tears, but he had a strange look in his eyes. His eyes were cold-like, full of hate. I don't know what came over him or Squeaky, Mrs. Graban, really I don't, but that's what happened." Cheryl had stopped crying and was feeling better now that she had someone to talk to about it. It frightened her; she had never seen Tommy act this like before.

Odell went up to Tommy's bedroom to talk to him and found him hiding in the corner of the room with Squeaky on his lap. His head was against the wall, eyes staring into an abyss with no sign of tears. Odell noticed his face was dry and it scared him. Had Tommy become cold and emotionless? There had to be some kind of feeling within him to do what he did downstairs.

"Tommy, please talk to me, or at least look at me. I want to help. Please let me help," Odell begged. Tommy still would not look at him. Tommy's condition had not changed; maybe it had even gotten worse. He hoped the psychiatrist might have a few answers for him. He didn't want to lose Tommy too. Odell was looking at Tommy, studying him for answers when the phone rang downstairs.

"Dear, it's for you," Betty yelled upstairs to her husband. "I think it's Agent Trimble."

Odell walked down the stairs slowly and somberly, thinking about Tommy and grabbed the phone. "Hello, this is Odell."

"Odell, this is Agent Trimble. I know it is a bad time to call, but we have to talk to you as soon as we can about the deaths.

Can you come down to the station tomorrow morning and meet with me and the Sheriff?"

"Yes, what time do you want me?" Odell, answered, knowing that he had no plans for quite some time.

"About nine okay with you?"

"Yea, I'll see you then," Odell answered and hung up without saying goodbye.

Josh tapped on the open door of Sheriff Bean's office. "Got a minute, Sheriff?" Agent Trimble asked as he walked in and sat down in a chair facing the Sheriff. "I've got Odell Graban coming in at nine o'clock tomorrow morning for an interview. Would you like to sit in?"

"Sure, I've got nothing scheduled tomorrow morning. I know Odell a lot better than you and maybe he will be more relaxed with me here. Odell has been under a lot of strain and he still is not himself. Hopefully we can melt some of that ice that has built up inside of him."

Odell didn't show up for his meeting until nine-thirty and apologized to both the Sheriff and Agent Trimble. "Sorry I'm late but I just have not been thinking right lately and my mind seems to wander off. I forget time and everything else."

"That's okay, Odell, we understand. Just have a seat here," Josh said, motioning to the seat next to him and in front of the Sheriff.

"Thanks for the help at the funeral, Sheriff. We are so relieved that the ground was not frozen yet and the bodies could be buried immediately and not have to wait until the spring thaw and go through the painful ordeal all over again. I don't think the pain will ever go away. I'm thinking about seeing a psychiatrist myself, which is something I never dreamed that I would have to do in my lifetime. I always thought that I was very stable and a strong man but this has brought me down to my knees."

Odell was finally opening up to someone so both Josh and the Sheriff let him continue without interrupting. Both felt this was good for Odell and hoped their meeting would bring Odell out of the shell he had put himself in.

"I've even stopped going to church," Odell continued. "I realized that God is not a God of love but a God of vengeance. It seems to me that all the good people have troubles and all the evil people just seem to get by with no problems. They always have money and never a care in the world. I mean, look at the drug dealers, our politicians and our crooked businessmen. They are all doing well and nothing ever happens to them. Why would God destroy a wonderful person like my daughter and her two lovely children? Even Tommy has been destroyed; his life will never be the same. Maybe someday I will get my faith back, but it won't be for a long time."

Odell suddenly became silent so the Sheriff took over and told Odell that he could relate to how he felt. "Odell, we are trying to piece this together and you know that there are a lot of puzzling things about this whole crime that we are having trouble with. Like, what do those calling cards left at the scene mean and why were the victims attacked in such a gruesome way? Can you help us in any way?" the Sheriff was half asking and half pleading in hopes of even finding one clue that could point them in a different direction.

"Sorry, I've seen those cards but I have never heard the word dooble in my life and I have no clue as to who could have done this. I can't believe it was Ben. I mean, he loved those kids as much as Mary did even though he didn't spend much time with them. He's just not a violent person. Don't get me wrong, he wasn't the best husband in the world but he never abused Mary or the kids. He liked to drink and he liked to chase women but that's about it. I would be very surprised if he was involved."

"Thanks, Odell, for your input, but we are going to have to bring Ben in for questioning anyway," Josh said matter of factly.

"You know where I can get a good used TV?" Odell asked. "You know, it is the funniest thing. We came home from the funeral and Tommy had thrown Betty's iron at the TV screen. I asked our babysitter, Cheryl, about it. She told us that Tommy was watching the funeral, got upset and picked up the iron and threw it at the TV. Another funny thing, Tommy's dog, Squeaky, well, he went wild when the funeral was on. Cheryl said he jumped at the TV several times and just kept barking and barking and wouldn't stop."

Josh had been slouched in his chair but when he had heard the story just told him he sat erect and looked at the Sheriff and then at Odell. "What did you say? That's very odd behavior, Odell. Do you think the murderer was in the church and both Tommy and Squeaky recognized him?"

"It's possible, I suppose. I just thought that Tommy was so distraught that he lost control, but I couldn't figure out why Squeaky lost control too. That was a puzzler to me," Odell answered realizing he might have offered a clue to the crime without knowing it.

Josh, recognizing that a new direction in the case had opened up for him, got up from his chair, lit a cigarette and started pacing, his mind once again racing at a thousand miles an hour. "Odell, we're going to get several copies of the video from the cable station and give you one of them. I want you to look at it very carefully and write down the names of everyone you recognize in the church. We may have something here, I'm not sure what, but we have got to start someplace."

The Sheriff sensed that the interview was over. Josh's mind had already left the room and was heading for the cable station. "I guess that will be all for today, Odell. We'll be in touch if anything comes up." The Sheriff got up from his chair the same time as Odell did and he escorted him out of the building. He patted him on the back, shook his hand and again told him that if there was anything he needed that he wasn't to hesitate to call him.

- 9 -

Josh's small office was located in the rear of the Sheriff's department. There was barely enough room for a chair, a desk, one bookcase, a filing cabinet, and his polygraph. It was all squeezed into a twenty foot by twenty foot space and the Special Agent was constantly having trouble maneuvering about. If he was giving a polygraph to a suspect, the situation became even worse. He was leaning back in his chair with his feet resting on the edge of his desk, hands cuffed behind his head and daydreaming. Tomorrow was Thanksgiving and he was thinking about what he would do on his four days off. He would spend the weekend with Marcie; he didn't know what she had planned but he knew a turkey was definitely in the picture. Marcie was a good cook and he could taste the meal already.

The Vikings were playing Detroit at the Metro dome and he had been given two tickets from a friend of his on the Bureau who was unable to attend. Marcie loved the Vikings; it was a one o'clock game and if all worked well they would be home in time for her delicious meal. Josh hadn't seen the Vikings play since they moved from the old Bloomington Stadium to their new location in downtown

Minneapolis and he was excited at the prospect of attending the game with Marcie.

Three weeks had quickly passed since the Helms' murders and he was getting frustrated and anxious about solving the case. He was frustrated that he was at a dead end in the case and anxious because for every day that went by, the odds narrowed in finding the killer. He was exhausted too; he was dividing his time between the Helms case and his court trial in Cedarton. It was time for a vacation. The four days off would renew and refresh him.

His thoughts of Marcie and the vacation vanished as fast as they had appeared. His mind quickly flashed back to the investigation and his bewilderment in the case. Nothing seemed to add up. He had interviewed everyone that was remotely connected to the Graban family and the Helms family, nothing. He felt like he was hitting his head against a brick wall. He interviewed Ben Helms and was certain that Ben had nothing to do with the murders. Ben did not fit any profile of a murderer. He was not very bright and was unwilling to accept any responsibilities for either himself or someone else, but he wasn't a killer. He had taken a polygraph test and had passed. Ben had been the only suspect Josh had; and with Ben practically eliminated, he was now up against another brick wall.

Tommy still was not talking and had sunken into a deeper catatonic state since he had watched the funerals and threw the iron at the television. If only Tommy would snap out of it; if he could talk and hopefully identify the killer. Josh was sure the killer knew the family and that Tommy provided the answers. He thought of Tommy hiding under the bed and not seeing anything, but he could have seen everything and that was why he was under the bed in a state of shock. Odell and Betty had taken their grandson to several psychiatrists, child psychologists, and post-traumatic experts with no luck. They had driven to the Twin Cities or Rochester with him almost every day in hopes that one of the doctors might break through the shell that Tommy had built around himself. Tommy was the answer, but why wasn't he killed? The killer had to have known he was there. Until Tommy regained himself, another dead end would remain just that.

Josh took his feet off the desk and slowly rose from his chair and maneuvered the short distance to his file cabinet. He opened the top drawer, pulled out the Helms file, and laid it in the middle of his uncluttered desk. He studied the file again, looking for something he might have missed. The report of the incident at the Grabans with Tommy and Squeaky offered some hope that Tommy could identify the killer. It was the only explanation; the killer had to have been in the church. He made a few copies of the video given to him by the cable company and asked Mary's friends and relatives of the family to view it, to study it and carefully look for any strangers that may have been in the church that day. It would have been a monumental task for Josh to get the video to everyone that attended the funeral but Frank and Tom volunteered to do that part of the investigation saving Josh hours of valuable time. Frank did most of the interviewing and hoped that at least one person would recognize an unfamiliar face in the church. Everyone who received the video studied it carefully and returned it to either Frank or Josh. No one was able to identify or could remember any strange face or person in the church that day. Even with no one recognizing a stranger at the funeral, the killer may be familiar to all of them without them even knowing it. Every time studied the file, he became more convinced the killer lived in Bishop or near Bishop. Josh put the file back into the cabinet, and decided to quit for the day. The weather report was good for the Thanksgiving weekend and Josh wouldn't have to worry about driving to the Twin Cities on snow packed roads. The forecasters informed the public that the Indian summer they were experiencing would last at least through the weekend. Josh was planning to have a good time with Marcie and would forget about the Helms family until he returned to work on Monday.

Josh showered, shaved, and dressed. He poured himself a cup of coffee, leaned against the kitchen counter of his small apartment, and slowly drank it. Marcie was expecting him in an hour and a half and he had plenty of time to get there. He met Marcie for the first time three months ago at Pete's Tavern. He wondered why he hadn't noticed her before; he thought he knew everyone in Bishop. He learned she moved to the small town a month ago from metro area. The crime and gang activity worried her and she yearned for a quieter town and a simpler lifestyle. It was time to leave Minneapolis she told him, she wanted out of the big city, discovered Bishop six months earlier, and decided this was where she wanted to live; it had everything she wanted. She quit her job as a legal secretary for a large law firm in Minneapolis, sub-leased her condo, and moved to Bishop. She easily found an apartment and a job doing the same work she had been doing in the Twin Cities. When they eventually met, Marcie and Josh discovered they had a lot in common. His stories of the cases he had worked on interested her and she found herself falling in love with this large, tanned and handsome BCA agent. They were soon more than friends and spent most weekends together. Marcie was not like his ex, she was interested and supportive of his work.

Josh carried his cup of coffee to his car and as he was about to open the car door he stopped, trying to remember if he shut off the stove. He walked back into the apartment as he had done many times before and checked the stove and the coffee pot and to make sure he had shut off all the lights. Everything was always turned off, but he checked anyway. He was half way out the door when he heard the phone ring. He stopped, turned around, and stared at the phone, deciding whether to answer it or not. He had a premonition that if he answered the phone his weekend would be ruined. He decided to let the answering machine take over. If it was somebody he should talk to, he would answer it. After the fourth ring, the voice came on.

"Josh, this is Sheriff Bean. I've...," Josh rushed over to the phone and picked it up hoping that Sheriff Bean would still be on the line.

"Yea, Sheriff, this is Josh." He pulled a cigarette out of his shirt pocket, lit it, and waited for the Sheriff to continue.

"We've got two more bodies, both women. They were found at Smith's quarry less than an hour ago by the owner of the gravel pit. A lot of similarities between these murders and the Helms murders, you better get out here. We've got the quarry roped off. How long before you can get here? I hope you didn't have any plans for the weekend."

"Yea, I did have plans this weekend but I'll cancel and be down in a couple of hours." Disappointed that his weekend with Marcie was ruined he slowly hung up the phone, wondering if he should have answered it. He called BCA headquarters and talked to the crime lab, briefly filling them in on what the Sheriff had told him. Walking to his car, he pulled out his cell, phoned Marcie, and filled her in on what he had to do. He apologized and promised he would make it up to her at Christmas.

Marcie hung up the phone and glanced around her kitchen wondering what she was going to do with all the food she was preparing for their special evening together. She hadn't experienced dating anyone in law enforcement before. Her previous dates were reliable and could be counted on to arrive at her house on time. She was learning that this relationship might be a little different.

A hard frost had hit the lower elevations hard the night before and the deep ruts in the gravel road to the quarry were frozen solid. Josh was thankful he had his seat belt on securely; otherwise, he would have been jostled around the car like an out of control gyroscope. The road to the bottom of the quarry was a half-mile long and by the time, he arrived at the crime scene he felt like everything had been shaken from his body. He looked in the rear view mirror, straightened his hair, and slowly got out of his car. He noticed four deputies were busy roping off the crime scene with yellow DO NOT CROSS plastic tape. An ambulance was parked next to one of the squad cars with its engine running, waiting to take the bodies to the hospital morgue.

"Who are they?" Josh asked the Sheriff as he walked toward him.

"Debbie Rawlings and Beth Anderson."

Josh walked to the older model El Camino and looked inside through the passenger window. Splatters of blood obscured his view so Josh opened the door, knelt down, and studied the grizzly scene in front of him. Both of the women had their throat slit in the same manner as the first three victims. A large amount of blood covered the victim's blouses and the car seat, and their hair hastily sheared off. Their mouths were half-agape and he noticed a plastic baggie had been pushed inside each of their mouths. Josh stood up, closed the door, looked at the Sheriff, and shrugged his shoulders.

"Look over here," Deputy Blume yelled to Josh, pointing to small pile of what looked like burned hair lying on the ground in back of the El Camino. "It looks like our killer put some of their hair in a pile and lit it on fire."

"Strange," Josh answered while studying the charred remains of what appeared to be human hair. "Put it in an evidence bag will you? You can sign it over to me later."

Josh took several photos of the crime scene before telling the EMT's they could leave. "We can't move the bodies until our investigative unit arrives; when they give me the word the bodies can be moved, I'll give you a call." Josh now knew for certain that he was dealing with an experienced and unstable serial killer. It was time to put the profiles of the murders on NCIC, National Crime

Information Center, and hopefully get a hit from some other area of the Country that was dealing with the same type of homicide or homicides. The killer was extremely clever and Josh was certain he had honed his craft long before the murders around Bishop. He had a serial killer on his hands and he now had to look at the murders in a completely different light. The killings didn't make sense and appeared to be random acts, which would make solving the case even harder. Josh walked the entire area of the gravel pit looking for clues but none were found. He would wait for the crime unit to arrive and offer his help. If he wasn't needed, he would go to his office and begin his reports.

The naked bodies of the two young women were lying on two stainless steel tables; a white linen cloth covered each of them. The autopsy was about to begin and the doctor, two RN's and the coroner were sitting in a little makeshift coffee room that abutted the morgue. They were waiting for Josh.

He arrived at the morgue as the pathology team were pouring their first cups of coffee; he was offered one and gladly accepted the invitation. Special Agent Trimble had witnessed many autopsies during his career with the Criminal Bureau of Apprehension and once told the Sheriff 'you seen one, you seen 'em all' but he knew that wasn't exactly true. The two autopsies didn't take as long as Josh had expected and he was glad of that. Satisfied he had all the needed information, he thanked the pathologist and his team and gathered his evidence, which included blood samples, fingernail scrapings, fingerprints of both girls, blood types, urine results and the plastic baggies that were taken from each of the girl's mouths; there were no semen samples to be gotten. He sat at a small metal desk near one of the steel tables and carefully opened the baggies and laid their contents on the desk. Inside each of the baggies was a calling card, similar looking to the ones found at the Helms murders. These murders were somehow connected, but why and how and what was the motive. If he could only figure that out, he would have a better chance of finding the killer. He needed to investigate further and discover if Debbie Rawlings and Beth Anderson were somehow connected to or knew Mary Helms.

Debbie Rawlings was the first victim and Josh arrived at that conclusion because of the sequence of the cards. Taken from her mouth was the all too familiar white calling card printed in calligraphy, 'DEATH. ON. OTHERS. B.L.E.' He carefully removed the second card from the baggie, the one that had been stuffed in Beth's mouth. It read 'DEATH. ON. OTHERS. BY. L.E.' He was convinced of the order of the deaths but would have to wait for the pathologists report to confirm it. He studied the cards; what did L.E. stand for and did those two remaining letters indicate two more murders were to take place? Both cards had been done in the same calligraphy style and the paper and style of ink appeared similar to the first three cards. Josh had completed his work and was waiting for the nurses to finish cleaning up the bodies. When they were thoroughly washed, he took a second and final look at the two corpses.

The head nurse for the hospital approached Josh as he was walking out of the morgue and informed him that Sheriff Bean was waiting in the conference room and wanted to talk with him. Josh thanked the nurse and asked where the conference room was. She pointed it out to him and he walked down a carpeted hallway until he found the room he was looking for and entered.

The Sheriff was sitting at the end of a long, narrow mahogany table. The Sheriff, unable to hide his emotions very well, had a look of obvious anxiety on his face. "Well?" he asked.

"Just got out of the morgue, the autopsies' done and I haven't had a chance to review any of the information yet. For certain, I can tell you that Debbie Rawlings and Beth Anderson were murdered by the same person that killed Mary Helms and her two children."

"How'd you come to that conclusion?"

"Because there were two calling cards left at the scene that match the ones left at the Helms house. The color of the card stock is the same, the material of the cards appears to be the same and the ink looks similar; their throats were slit and their hair was cut off. The guy is going to kill again and we need to get him before he does. I've taken all the specimens I needed and also a couple dozen pictures at the autopsy. I'll upload them for you when I get back to the office."

"It's been almost a couple of months between the Helms' murders and these murders; the killings were what, a couple of miles apart. Guy's got to live around here and maybe even in the area of the killings. I'll check for all newcomers to the county within the last year. I'll sleep much better when this guy is caught," the

Sheriff said as he got up from his comfortable chair, ready to leave. "I'll meet you back at the office."

Josh stared out the narrow triple pane window that overlooked Main Street from his office. He was listening to Vivaldi's 'Four Seasons'. The Sheriff poked his head into Josh's office, appearing to enjoy the music. "How's it going?" the Sheriff asked.

"Great." Josh replied while studying the Sheriff, trying to get an indication of his mood. "As long as you're here, I need to ask you a favor. Can you spare me another deputy besides Frank? I'm going to need a lot of leg work done and I would like to have Tom Jenks brought into help. I like the way he works and he does have a vested interest in the case."

"I can't see a problem. We'll have to pay some overtime but I don't think the county board will mind, but why Tom? He is still distraught over the deaths of Mary and the kids. Do you really think that is a wise idea? Besides that, he is still a rookie and has no investigative experience. What if he screws something up for you?" the Sheriff questioned, but offered Josh all the help he needed. He just wanted this thing solved.

"Thanks, Sheriff, and I know your concerns about Tom, but I think we can use him. He wants the killer worse than anyone else on the department and he will work harder than anyone else to solve it. He may be taking some of this personally and it may affect his judgment but I really don't think so. What the hell, this might bring him out of his depression. Can the four of us meet in your office tomorrow morning and review what we have so far?"

"No problem, I'll contact Frank and Tom and we'll see you in the morning. I'm taking off; hope the rest of your day goes better.'

The next morning at nine o'clock, the investigative team with its newest member was gathered in the Sheriff's office. An open box of donuts, sitting on the corner of the Sheriff' desk was inviting and tempting and before long all members of the team were eating a glazed donut and drinking a cup of coffee. Everyone was occupied with drinking their coffee and eating their donut and there was a lull in the conversation; the Sheriff thought it would be a good time to start the meeting. He began by scribbling something on a note pad in front of him and without saying anything, he held up the piece of paper up. "See this word." The Sheriff said as he pointed his index finger to the word he had written down. "Do you know this word?" They all said they were very familiar with the word dooble. "This word, dooble, is going to be the name of the file on this case. Anything you hear or find regarding this case is to be entered into the computer titled DOOBLE. Study the file often and then read it again, hopefully something new will pop into those heads of yours and we can catch ourselves a killer."

Josh took over the meeting and began by displaying the calling card that was found on Beth Anderson. "I have no idea what these calling cards are going to spell out, if I did we would name the case differently but I hope we never get the opportunity to find out what the last two letters on the card stands for because that would mean there have been two more murders."

"Dooble?" Frank said, more a question than a statement. "Makes sense to me, it's probably the piece of evidence that is going to lead us to our killer."

"That is all I could come up with, if anybody has a better idea let's hear it." None of the team offered anything better and the room was silent. "Yes Frank," the Sheriff answered. "The calling cards are the one thing that definitely connects all five murders. The modus operandi of the killer is the same in all five killings; tells us he's got to be the same person." In complete detail, the Sheriff covered all five of the murders, the evidence, the time of deaths, and all other pertinent information the two deputies needed. Most of the information was new to them and they wrote it down in their notebooks and then reviewed their notes for questions; there were none.

"As you know, there are not many clues, but I need your help in tracking down anything you can find to make these clues work," Josh said, taking over the conversation while the Sheriff was getting himself another cup of coffee. "Frank, I need you to check out every printing company in a fifty mile area and any websites that specialize in calligraphy equipment. I need to know if any of their customers had purchased similar pens or inks recently or if anyone bought business cards similar to the paper quality of the ones found at the scene." Josh passed around the calling card taken from Beth Anderson's mouth. It was sealed in a plastic evidence bag but the card was clearly visible to the viewer.

"This is the most important piece of evidence we have so far. Frank, I need to know which paper companies sell this type of bond paper and I want to know who their customers are in Minnesota. I'm guessing our killer buys all his equipment at the same place. His calligraphy is excellent so we can be sure he isn't a novice at this and has been doing it for quite some time."

With a full cup of coffee in hand, the Sheriff leaned back in his chair and fondled his chin. He reached behind him and punched the intercom switch that went directly to his secretary and asked her to come into the office and make another pot of coffee. "You guys both know you are being taken out of the squad for the time being until this case is solved. Your only job for now will be working on dooble. I've gotten the authorization from the County Board for overtime for the other deputies and for you guys. They want this thing solved as badly as we do and are willing to compromise some tax dollars to do it."

"Tom," Josh said, looking at Deputy Jenks, "You're familiar with video equipment, right?"

Tom paused for a second before answering, wondering what Josh had in mind. "Yea, Josh, I do a lot of video work, but only as a hobby, why?"

"Monday is the funeral for the girls. I want you to video both funerals. I want an extensive video. I want you to scan the congregation over and over again and from every angle possible. I also want you to scan the entire church in case someone is watching apart from the congregation. I want at least a dozen copies made; put them on my desk when you're done. I am pretty sure our killer was at the Helms' funeral and will be at these two also. Give each of us a copy right away, the other copies I won't need for a couple of days. We'll study the videos individually and then collectively, see with what we come up with. Can you do that, Tom?"

"Yes, but I am going to look conspicuous, aren't I?"

"Uh huh, but I don't think you will have many questions, if you do I am sure you will think of something to say." Josh answered.

Frank looked at the Sheriff, "What are the times of the funerals?"

"The funeral director called from the funeral home and he has given us the times. It looks like the service for Debbie Rawlings will be at 10:30 A.M. and Beth's will be at 2:00. Both girls belonged to the Abundant Life Church. I sure feel sorry for Pastor Bartholomew. He has gone through quite a lot with the Helms' funerals and now two more violent deaths."

"That's quite a coincidence, isn't it?" Tom asked.

"Not really," Josh answered. "That church has the largest congregation in Bishop and I heard that half the town belongs to that church."

Sheriff Bean got up to pour himself another cup of coffee and offered another cup to Josh, Tom, and Frank. He asked if there were any questions so far and all three stated they didn't have anything further to ask right now. Sheriff Bean quickly downed his last cup of coffee for the morning and informed the group he had to drive to Cedarton for a sheriff's sale and would be in touch. The two deputies and Josh hung around the office finishing their coffee and talking about the case, all of them anxious to get to work. Tom had been asked by Josh to check the shoe stores in Bishop and Cedarton to see if the soles of the sandals found imprinted at the Helms' murder scene were familiar to any of the clerks at the stores. Josh also wanted to know if any of the salespeople at the stores could remember anybody in particular who wore sandals most of the time. Both Tom and Frank had work to do and said their goodbyes to Josh, leaving their coffee cups on the Sheriff's desk for the secretary to remove and wash.

Josh sat alone in the office staring at the "Citizen of the Year" award that the Sheriff had received last year. He lit a cigarette and was thinking that it was a smart idea to bring Tom and Frank into the case. Maybe they would stumble onto something that would break the case open.

- 10 -

Pastor Bartholomew pulled a metal plated Zippo lighter from his right vest pocket and placed it carefully on his mahogany desk. From the top drawer of his desk he retrieved a cigarillo. Acting as if this was some sort of ceremonial rite to be performed he picked up the Zippo, looked admiringly at the bold JPB gold lettering on its front and flicked it open with his thumb. He spun the little wheel triggering the flint which instantly created a yellow, orange, and blue flame. He set the lighter on the desk and stared at the flame while carefully unwrapping the cellophane from the cigar. He crumpled the cellophane wrapper and deposited it in the wastebasket under the desk. He put the cigarillo in his mouth and leaned toward the lighter carefully placing the tip of the cigarillo in the flame until it was lit and then passionately inhaled the smoke. He closed the lighter, lifted it off the desk, and returned it to his vest pocket.

The Pastor got up and paced back and forth in front of his behemoth desk, which took up a good portion of his office. It was the same routine every week as he prepared his Sunday sermon. It set the mood. This week though, he had two eulogies to prepare beside his Sunday sermon. The eulogies were going to be tough because he hardly knew either of the dead girls. He knew who they were and that was about all. He was aware Debbie Rawlings was a member of the church and Beth Anderson had applied for membership but they seldom attended. He remembered the Sunday morning that Debbie brought a friend with her to church. They talked briefly after the service and Debbie introduced her friend and told him that her friend Beth was seriously considering joining the church. That was one of the last times he had seen Beth. He couldn't remember much about her except she was living in Cedarton when he talked to her and heard she had moved to Bishop shortly after that. He recalled that she and Debbie shared an apartment above the bank. Debbie was working at the Jones Insurance Agency and Beth was looking for work. That was all he knew about them.

The last time he could remember talking to them was when they walked into his office unexpectedly one morning while he was working on his sermon. Without saying a word, they calmly walked over to two overstuffed French provincial chairs facing his desk. They sat down and quietly looked at him, waiting for some kind of recognition. He was smoking his cigarillo and studying some notes he had written down. He scornfully looked at them, angry they had intruded on his space without even an apology. Debbie Rawlings began the conversation by telling the pastor that her friend Beth Anderson had decided to join the church. She assured the pastor that they would be more faithful in attending church in the future and apologized for not coming more often. Debbie paused, waiting for a reaction from Pastor Bartholomew; she studied his face searching for some kind of an expression or reaction to give them some idea of how he felt about the matter. His face looked stern and was without emotion and that confused both girls as they silently looked at each other and shrugged. They were in his office only a short time when Beth suddenly got up from her chair and placed her application to become a member of the church on his desk. Both women quickly left without saying another word. When they were gone he picked up the application, read it and laid it back down on his desk; he would check it further when he had time.

Pacing back and forth, he was thinking of the girls, their awful murders and how he was going to tie everything into the eulogies. He stopped in front of the mirror and his mind wandered to other things.

The mirror was one of his lucky finds. He found it at a garage sale and paid five dollars and the Pastor sensed the seller was relieved to see it go. The frame was painted lime green, a retro color popular in the 40's and which he did not like. He took it home, stripped the paint off, and discovered that the frame was a beautiful dark cherry. After refinishing the frame with two coats of varnish, he brought it to his office. The mirror stood a full six-foot high. There were actually two mirrors, a dowel in the middle of the framework allowed the mirror to rotate and reveal a similar mirror on the other side. The one side was a regular mirror, reflecting the actual size of the person facing it, but the other side allowed the viewer to look much taller than he was. This is the side the pastor liked. He was five foot eight and all his life yearned to be taller. The mirror allowed him to realize for a brief time his fantasy. He stood in front of the mirror as he often did and looked at himself in contempt. His hair, now mostly gray, was visible only on the side of his head while the top was completely bald except for a few strands of curly thin hair that were still left. His reddish complexion made him look like he was suffering from a bad case of high blood pressure and that he would blow up at almost anytime. He tried getting his skin to tan; he went on vacations to sunny places and tried tanning booths but the texture of his skin never changed. His thick glasses made his eyes appear to be bulging out of their sockets and his paunch stomach revealed a lack of exercise. He had tried exercising once but quickly realizing it was too much work and took too much dedication so he quit. He stood there, looked at his reflected image, and cursed God under his breath for creating him the way he had.

In September, he turned forty-seven years old. Pastor John Paul Bartholomew had been a minister half of his life. He had graduated from the seminary in Stonebrake, Illinois and had served in four congregations before being called to the Abundant Life Church. The previous pastor, Alfonso Crumb, had been the founder and leader of the Abundant Life Church for over forty years. At eighty-one, the distinguished, silver-haired, sensible, and prudent leader had died in his sleep, leaving the church without a pastor. Pastor Crumb had on many occasions urged the church fathers to hire an assistant pastor to help him with his duties and allow him to train a person to take over the congregation when he either retired or died. They had listened dutifully, promised they would, but never got around to it. The church council hastily began their search for a replacement and found it in Pastor Bartholomew. One of the church council members had visited a congregation in Ypsilanti, Michigan and heard Pastor Bartholomew speak. He was impressed and submitted his name to the council. The council posthaste sent a letter of call to Pastor Bartholomew.

Without hesitation, he accepted the call to Bishop. He was uncomfortable with the congregation in Ypsilanti and was tired of their constant meddling into his personal life. They were always questioning him about what he was doing on his days off and were always asking why they couldn't get a hold of him. They were nitpicky about everything he did at the church and especially curious and suspicious of his private life. He wanted out; he wanted a smaller church and a quieter life.

He liked Bishop and realized that as a newcomer to the town, it would take a while for the townspeople to warm up to him but knew he would eventually be accepted. The town offered him everything he was looking for and he was convinced he would remain in Bishop for the rest of his life.

He had been the church's leader for almost six months and the congregation still had not warmed up to him. He knew he would have a difficult time at first, he always did. The congregation was comfortable with Pastor Crumb and his ways and still weren't ready for a change nor did they accept change easily. He wasn't adored by the members of the congregation but he wasn't disliked either. He just seemed to be there but wasn't able to bring out the real feelings of the members of the church in regards to him or his personality. The reason may have been that he had the same feelings for the human race. He neither adored people nor hated them. He had kind of a "take me or leave me" attitude and it reflected to those around him. Because of his feeling toward people and of those toward him, he had become a loner. He was seldom seen with anyone and the only time he seemed to enjoy anybody's company was when he was at the Bishop Cafe each morning for the local coffee clutch meetings. The conversations were usually intelligent and it seemed that at least there, at that small table in that small Cafe, someone seemed to care what he had to say on subjects other than religion.

Bartholomew was a freshman in college when the Army Reserve arrived early one morning at his campus. A makeshift booth was set up in front of Main Hall; the Army was on campus for their annual recruiting drive. The drab green kiosk caught the attention of the young Bartholomew as he walked by on his way to a class. He stopped and visited with the Sergeant manning the booth; and before Bartholomew walked away, he had filled out an application. The Army life, with its discipline and order interested him and when he was accepted into the Reserves, it was one of the happiest days of his life.

When he arrived in Bishop to take over the duties of pastoring the Abundant Life Church, he was still a member of the Reserves just like his brother. The Army Reserves had become a big part of his life, maybe even more so than his other job. The local Reserves were headquartered in Cedarton and he transferred to that unit as soon as he moved to Bishop. When he was interviewed for the job, he informed the church council at Abundant Life that he was a member of the Reserves and they would have to make allowances for a few weekends off a year. The council had no problem with Bartholomew's Army responsibilities; in fact, they hired an intern to assist him with the congregation. The council did not want to be left without a pastor again.

He discovered he was gay when he was sixteen years old. In those days, he would have been called a faggot or a queer and the discrimination against him would have been so intense he wouldn't have been able to handle it. He kept his homosexuality hidden and still had not come out of the closet. His homosexuality confused him. In the eyes of God he knew it was a sin but in his eyes it didn't seem all that wrong. He wanted so much to come out of the closet but knew that by revealing it, his career as a pastor would come to an abrupt end and he certainly would be kicked out of the Reserves. To solve this dilemma, he carried on a secret life. He knew he couldn't get romantically involved with another man because that could lead to serious emotional problems and might bring his homosexuality too much into the open. His answer to this dilemma was realized years ago and he was following the same pattern of secrecy in Minnesota as he had in Ypsilanti. He would drive to Minneapolis which proved to be a good replacement for Ypsilanti every Tuesday night and frequent the Sterling Horse where he would pick up a male prostitute. Wednesday was his day off and nobody would think anything of his being gone Tuesday evening and part of Wednesday. They would just assume he needed to get out of town for a while and relax. He successfully carried out this routine for the last twenty years and no one had found him out yet. There was no emotional attachment and he could get the sexual satisfaction he needed although the guilt was always there.

Tired of looking at himself in the mirror the pastor sat down behind his desk and deeply inhaled the last puff from his cigar before snuffing it out in the ashtray. He removed a Kleenex from his desk drawer and wiped the ash tray clean over his wastebasket. He looked at the words he had written down on the piece of paper, then crumpled up the piece of paper and threw it into his wastebasket and began again. The eulogies would be difficult to write; he had no idea what to say. He decided it would be a generic sermon; he would give a brief biography of the women, mention their relatives and talk about the wicked times we live in and wind it up with a discourse on faith. He would use the Book of Revelation as his guide and to make his point about how evil is going to take over the world and reign supreme in the last days.

He finished the eulogies in less than an hour. It had gone faster then expected but once he determined a theme it went fast. He reread the eulogies and was pleased with what he had written. He decided to put off writing his Sunday's sermon until Thursday. He methodically rose from his desk, removed his winter coat from the coat rack, put it on, walked to his car, and began his one-hour drive to Minneapolis.

- 11 -

A week after Thanksgiving the weather around Bishop turned dismal. A blanket of clouds covered the sky, dampness permeated the air, and the temperature had dropped to the mid twenties. It was a gloomy backdrop for the funerals. The previous week had brought Indian summer throughout the Thanksgiving weekend but then the weather changed, signaling the beginning of the long winter that was to lie ahead. The sudden cold snap that abruptly arrived in the area caused the ground to harden with a light layer of frost and the pastor was worried that there might not be a burial. The bodies might have to be interred in a cemetery vault until spring.

A handful of people attended the Debbie Rawlings funeral; Beth Anderson's funeral attracted even fewer. Although Debbie Rawlings had been a life long resident of Bishop and everyone knew her from the insurance agency, she never developed 'real' friends or got to know the locals very well. It was her fault, she didn't feel like she fit into the Bishop 'scene'. Her best friend was herself and she never developed a real kinship with town. The Helms funeral had taken a lot out of the people of Bishop and they weren't ready for another one so shortly afterwards. Beth did not know a soul in town except for Debbie; the only people that attended her funeral were immediate family and a few close friends from Cedarton. Deputy Tom Jenks filmed both funerals from different angles and distances zooming in on the faces of everyone in attendance. His job had become much easier after taking a head count. He thought more people would be at the funerals; where were the curiosity seekers?

The editing of the video would take time and be quite boring. On his way home from the church he stopped at a local mini-mart and picked up a case of beer and some junk food thinking that he might as well have some fun while performing his duties and getting paid overtime to do them. When he arrived at his small apartment, he unloaded the case of beer in the refrigerator, leaving one out for himself. He opened a can of Spanish peanuts and uncapped his beer. He booted his computer, sat down in front it, and began the tedious job of editing and copying the video. He vigilantly studied the computer screen as the camera scanned the church from all angles. While editing the video he noticed for the first time the face of one of the people leaving church after the Rawlings funeral. It was not a person he recognized and he was surprised he hadn't picked up on it while he was filming. He backed the video to the beginning and started it. A few minutes into the filming, he noticed that the same man he saw walking out of the church was the same man that was sitting in the front pew on the left side of the church.

The first three rows of pews on the right side were reserved for family and roped off prior to the service. Although they were reserved, only a handful of people occupied the first row, leaving two rows empty. Tom knew Debbie's family and would contact them later. He needed to know if anyone of them recognized the man sitting on the opposite side of them.

After the unexpected discovery of the stranger, Tom viewed the film in slow motion. The first image of him was sitting alone in the front pew. He sat erect, stoic, and motionless, only once lifting his arm to wipe one of his eyes. During the service, the stranger never took his eye off the pastor and appeared to be listening intently to what he was saying. The pastor must have noticed the stranger also as he looked at him briefly on several occasions. After the funeral, he simply got up with the rest of the congregation and quietly walked out of the church and disappeared. Tom had gotten good footage of him leaving the church and studied his facial features, mannerisms, and dress. He was sure he would run into him again and wanted to recognize him when he did.

Watching the second funeral Tom noticed that the same man attended the second funeral and sat in the same pew and as before, again watching the pastor intently. His excitement was almost more than he could contain. He went to a small bookcase above his television and pulled out the DVD of the Helms' funerals. He slipped it into his computer and began watching it, hoping to find the same stranger. When the camera panned the front three rows of the church Tom spotted the stranger sitting in the same place he had when he attended both the Rawlings funeral and the Anderson funeral. He realized how he and everybody else watching the film had missed him. The back of his head, with the way his hair was combed, looked exactly like Bobbie Williams. It was an easy mistake except this person wore an earring in his left ear and Bobbie Williams would not be caught dead with an earring in his ear. Tom looked at his watch, it was still early enough to call the Sheriff and let him know what he had discovered. On the third ring, the Sheriff answered.

"Sheriff, this is Tom. I think I might have found our killer."

"Tom, slow down, what are you talking about?"

"You aren't gonna' believe this but at each of the funerals there was somebody there that I have never seen. I am sure you haven't either. I've got him on film at all the funerals and at each one, he's sitting in the same pew. We gotta have a meeting; I gotta show this to you."

"Tom, that's unbelievable. Are you sure?"

"Absolutely. I've watched it over and over and this person ain't from anywhere around here. I'll promise you that."

"Okay, I'll get a hold of the others and we'll meet in my office tomorrow morning. Good work, Tom. You better get some sleep now. It is almost eleven and we'll see you tomorrow morning. Goodnight."

Tom was too excited to sleep so he put on his headphones, turned on his iPod and listened to one of his favorite groups, the Grateful Dead. He drank two more beers before falling asleep on his worn leather recliner.

After hearing the news from the Sheriff, the team arrived at the Law Enforcement Center a half an hour early, excited to view the video. They sat in the coffee room with a few of the other officers making small talk and discussing the arrests of the previous night and the dirtballs they had to deal with on a regular basis. At nine o'clock, they noticed the Sheriff unlock his office door and walk in. The three members of the dooble team simultaneously got up and walked to the Sheriff's office. The Sheriff called his secretary and asked her to come to his office. He needed his computer prepared to watch the DVD's of the funerals. The Sheriff was computer illiterate and was happy to have a secretary who was the opposite. In less time than it took her to make a pot of coffee, she had the computer ready to go.

Everyone watched her leave and then offered their "good mornings" to the Sheriff as Tom put the DVD of the Rawlings and Anderson funerals into the computer. Tom hadn't told them what to look for and as they watched the DVD of both funerals, none of the team noticed anything out of the ordinary. The second time he played the DVD, he pointed out the unfamiliar person sitting in the front pew. After the DVD was finished, he ejected it and inserted the DVD of the Helms funeral. He had everyone's interest when he started the second DVD. He paused it when the video scanned the back of the front pew on the left side of the church. He pointed out the man in the front row who appeared to be the same person at the other two funerals.

"But that's Bobbie Williams," Frank said while carefully studying the back of the stranger's head.

"Knowin' Bobbie Williams, Frank, would you say that he is kind of a redneck?" Tom asked.

"Ya, the biggest red-neck I've ever known," Frank answered while still looking at the video and trying to observe the man he thought was Williams.

"Look at his left ear, Frank." Tom said as he pointed to the small diamond earring in the stranger's ear. "Would Bobbie Williams ever wear an earring? I thought it was Bobbie Williams at first too because the hair on the stranger is the same color and the same style as Bobbie's."

"You're right," Josh added, looking at the video with a renewed interest. "Looks like Bobbie Williams has a twin."

"It was an easy mistake to make and we all did it, Josh. But I don't understand how someone with your training and experience could have missed something that obvious! When I think of what the State of Minnesota pays you, I just get sick. I mean even a rookie like Tom here was able to figure it out. I hope the entrance exams are harder now than when you got on," Milo jokingly said and smiled at Josh.

"Screw you, Sheriff," Josh replied as he scratched his chin with his middle finger aiming it at the Sheriff.

With the joking over, the Sheriff took over the meeting. There was a good chance they might have found the killer. But, who was he? Where would they start as no one in the room had ever seen this person. Where was he from? The Sheriff asked to have all of the frames showing the stranger blown up to eight by tens and have copies sent to all law enforcement agencies in Iowa, Michigan, Wisconsin, North and South Dakota and, of course, Minnesota. Someone in another department might recognize the stranger and at least provide a name.

"All of you keep your eyes open. Maybe, with a little luck, he is living right here in Bishop and we can spot him. Frank, how are you coming on locating people that have moved to the area recently?" the Sheriff asked.

"I got a list of twenty-seven people but I haven't followed up on them yet," Frank replied.

"Also, Frank, did you have any luck with your follow-up on the calligraphy?"

Frank stated that the only thing he had accomplished so far was to get a list of businesses in the surrounding area and the Twin Cities that sold calligraphy equipment and paper. He added that he studied several websites and was planning on contacting them today. "I'll be calling on the businesses next week. Who knows, I might get lucky like Tom did," Frank answered the Sheriff, wishing he had more information for him.

Tom added that he had checked several of the shoe stores in the area for anything resembling the soles of the sandals worn at the Helms' murder scene. Not only did he have no luck, but none of the stores sold sandals or anything resembling them. "It seems that sandals are not in real demand in this area at this time of the year. Plus, most people just didn't like the looks of sandals. That's kind of a dead end issue right now, but I'll keep pursuing it. I just wish we could have gotten a full picture of that guy at the church to see if he was wearing sandals."

"I'll tell you what I want you to do, Tom. Contact the two people that sat on each side of this guy at the Helms funerals. See if anyone recollects anything about him and if they remember if this guy was wearing sandals," the Sheriff said as he gave out assignments for the next meeting. "Josh, what've you got going on?"

"The first thing I'm going to do is get a hold of Odell Graban. I want to show the films of the last two funerals to Tommy and Squeaky and see what kind of reaction I get. I'm also going to spend a few days at the office in St. Paul going over mug shots and comparing them with the pictures of our stranger."

"Well, we've actually accomplished a lot these last few days. We might at least be working in the right direction. It's more than we had last week so the meeting is adjourned and let's get some serious police work done," the Sheriff joked once again. He patted Tom on the back acknowledging that he was happy with what Tom had discovered.

- 12 -

Entering the parking lot of the Sheriff's Department he did a half U-turn maneuver carefully backing his 1967 Yellow Mustang Mach 1 into the stall clearly marked STATE CRIME BUREAU PARKING ONLY. He turned off the powerful V-8 engine that had been idling so perfectly under the hood and looked into the rear view mirror checking that his neatly combed hair was still in place and adjusted his pastel colored tie. He looked at his watch, it was ten-thirty.

"Right on time," he said softly to himself.

Unless the Sheriff had a nine o'clock meeting schedule, which seemed to be happening a lot lately he was in his office between ten-thirty and eleven. Josh Trimble's body clock kept him up until after midnight and in bed until eight-thirty or nine in the morning. It had been that way for as long as he could remember. The only time that changed was when he was in the Corps. Getting up at five in the morning was the hardest thing about being a Marine, but he survived, albeit grudgingly.

He was a man of routine and a man who did not accept change easily. He had been forced to sacrifice some of his habits when he married Marilyn. Now that the marriage was behind him, he reverted back to the life he was accustomed to.

His days were definitely not routine, each one being different and offering a new adventure. After all those years with his wife, he finally developed a pattern in his life he was happy with. Now that Marcie had entered the picture, he knew he would have to give a little. He realized it and felt comfortable with it. She was a great lady and he didn't want to lose her. Besides, she seemed to understand and accept crazy hours involved with his work. His weekends were now being taken up with Marcie. They did many things together; they went shopping together, went to ball games together, went hiking together and every weekend Marcie cooked at least one meal at her apartment. Her cooking satisfied his Midwest male cravings of meat, potatoes, and a vegetable with a store bought pie topping it all off. Yes, Josh Trimble was a happy man, probably as happy as he had ever been in his life.

Satisfied that he looked presentable, he got out of his car and walked toward the red brick building that housed the Sheriff's department. As he was about to enter the building Sheriff Bean was walking out the door and met him.

"Mornin' Sheriff," Josh said, tossing his half smoked cigarette into the sand filled ashtray that stood beside the front door.

Sheriff Bean stopped and held the glass door open for Josh.

"Good morning Josh, just the man I've been looking for. Have you got time for a quick cup, I need to talk to you about something important."

Josh looked at his watch and decided that whatever he had to do could wait. "Sure Sheriff, where do you want to go?"

"I'll meet you at the Bishop Cafe in about fifteen minutes. I got some papers to drop off at the County Attorney's office first," he replied as he started walking toward his patrol car.

"See you in fifteen then," Josh turned around, walked back to his car and drove to the Bishop Cafe. When he got there, the parking lot was almost full but he managed to find a spot near the back door of the restaurant. He waited outside the front door for the Sheriff. A few minutes later he spotted the Sheriff's squad car pull into the lot just as another car was leaving. The Sheriff's squad quickly pulled into the empty parking space near the front door, got out of his car and greeted Josh once again with a "Good morning".

Before they entered the restaurant, the Sheriff stated he wanted to get a booth and hoped there was one available because he wanted to talk in private. Josh spotted an empty booth near the far end of the restaurant and nudged the Sheriff. The Sheriff noticed the booth and both aimed for it with a direct purpose in mind - getting there before someone else did. They reached the booth, quickly sat down on the outside edge of the booth, and faced each other. This left no room for anyone to sit down and intrude on their conversation. It was an accepted practice at the cafe and the customers knew what it meant.

Noticing her two newest customers, Dolly came over, picked up the dirty dishes, and heartily wiped the top of the table. She left as quickly as she had appeared and returned with two cups of coffee and placed them on the tabletop. "Anything else today?"

"What have you got for rolls?" the Sheriff asked.

Dolly looked toward the pastry display and then back at her customers. "All I've got left is pecan rolls. Would you boys like one?"

"I'll have one," the Sheriff answered and looked at Josh. "How about you?"

"Yea bring me one also and throw a couple of pads of butter in with it," Josh replied.

Dolly brought the two rolls and set them down in front of her customers, filled out her guest check and laid it in the middle of the booth for whoever was going to pay the bill.

"Anything new on the dooble murders?" the Sheriff asked trying the start the conversation that would lead into what he wanted to tell Josh.

"Nothing." Josh answered, blowing on his coffee to cool it off before he could take his first sip.

"What I really want to talk to you about isn't related to the investigation. I want to talk a little about my future. See, I've been thinking long and hard about my job since the Halloween storm and the Helms' murders. I've decided to hang it up; I'm going to retire after the first of next year. I mean, look at it, I'm sixty-two years old and I'm feeling the stress that has been thrown at me this last month. I can't sleep, I'm getting a nervous stomach, and I am not eating right. I think the strain is getting to me. I guess what I am saying is that a younger man would be able to handle the work and the pressures of the job better than me. I want to quit and appoint you as the Sheriff."

"What?" Josh looked the Sheriff in the eyes. He noticed that his dark cobalt eyes had a tired look to them. He had not noticed them until the Sheriff mentioned how he felt. He had always thought the Sheriff was untiring but now for the first time realized the Sheriff was looking old and fallible. "I had no idea you felt this way. I know you're tired from what's happened but it will soon be over and things will get back to normal. Why don't you hold off until your term of Sheriff is over and then make your decision? You love law enforcement; it's been your life. I think you would be a lonely man without it. I think you better do some more soul searching before you make a major decision like this."

"No, I've done all the soul searching, as you put it, that I am going to do. I've got thirty-two years under my belt and would be able to draw a nice pension. No, Josh, I've made up my mind and it cannot be changed. It has always been easy being Sheriff because nothing ever happened much in Davis County. Life has been nice and simple but that has all changed within the last few weeks and I think the simple life is gone forever. Things are changing so fast in the world that they are finally going to hit home here in Davis County. Look at Cedarton. The drug problem is getting out of hand over there and they have at least one burglary a night. I remember the days when there was maybe one burglary a year and it would make the front page of the Cedarton Chronicle; now it's third page news. It is going to filter down to Bishop eventually. I am just tired of all the shit nowadays with the liberal court systems and the State telling me how to run my jail and the crime and the drugs. I mean, look at my jail; it is more like a hotel than a punishment center. I mean, we arrest these pukes, they go to court, they are released, and a week later we have to arrest them all over again."

"That's called job security," Josh interrupted briefly.

"I've already got the job security," the Sheriff replied. "No, Josh, I have thought long and hard about this decision. I'm resigning and I want you to take over."

Without answering the Sheriff, he lifted his cup and took a sip of coffee. "That's too bad caus' I'm sure gonna' miss you. We go back a long ways and had a lot of fun together." Josh said, reminiscing. "Remember the time that you and Martha and Marilyn and I went to Las Vegas? I still chuckle about that. I'll never forget it. I know Martha still gets mad when she thinks about that elevator ride. We were on the fourth floor, of the Golden Nugget, remember, and all of us were taking the elevator down. We were going to get off at the second floor to make dinner reservations and meet the girls on the main floor. I remember the elevator was full of people. As we were getting off on the second floor, we thanked our wives for the fun night but said that we thought the $100 was a bit too much for what we got. The elevator door then closed with Martha and Marilyn left with an elevator full of all these strangers who were all staring at them. They didn't see the humor in what we did. They said they could feel the eyes of the passengers staring through them all the way down to the first floor."

As they sat and reminisced a little, Josh's thoughts went back to the career and life that the Sheriff had lived. He was born and raised in Bishop and after graduation got a few odd jobs around town before being drafted and sent to Vietnam. After his tour of duty was over, he came back to Bishop and took work wherever he could get it. He had been doing odd jobs around town when Sheriff Hans Brown offered him a job as deputy sheriff. He had been a deputy only two years when Sheriff Brown died unexpectedly of a heart attack. He was appointed by the County Board to fill his term and had been the Sheriff of Davis County ever since. He knew Milo and Martha wanted to have children, but it wasn't to be. Law enforcement kind of took the place of children for him.

"Well?" the Sheriff asked, part questioning, part pleading and part out of curiosity at how Josh was responding to the sudden news. "Will you give it some consideration?"

"I'll think about it and that's all I can say, you have to look at my situation, Sheriff. I make more money than you do, I have the freedom to set my own work schedule, and I don't have the headaches you have. Why would I want to change that?"

"Simple, you have lived here all your life and you could be doing the county a big favor by taking the job. I know about the money and all that but there is more to this job than money. You would have some prestige and power in the position. You would have all those conventions to go to and next year the National

Sheriff's Convention is being held in Hawaii. That could be something to look forward to. Think of it as a duty that you are fulfilling for the citizens of the county." The Sheriff answered, talking like a used car salesman trying to convince his customer to trade his car in for one of lower value.

"Like I said, I'll think about it," Josh replied. He took the last sip from his coffee and set the cup gently on the tabletop. "What about Frank? He's been with you a long time, the people like him and he knows the ins and outs of the department."

"Frank's my second choice, I am sure he will accept my offer if you don't. It will be a step up for him, although I don't know how long he is going to live with the lifestyle he's leading. I mean, I almost expect him to drop over from a heart attack any day."

Josh chuckled thinking of Frank and his health habits which had become a standing joke in the department. "You're probably right about that; we wouldn't want another situation like Hans Brown," Josh had decided he wanted to change the topic of conversation. "You going down to the Elks tonight for some poker?"

"Yea," the Sheriff answered and looked at his empty cup of coffee. He waived to Dolly indicating they would like refills. The Sheriff was about to continue when he heard a voice from behind him that sounded somewhat familiar although he couldn't put a face with the voice.

"Good morning, gentlemen," the man said as he stood in front of the booth facing them both. Josh noticed the man standing there was wearing an Army uniform, decorated with Captain's bars.

108

His uniform was neatly pressed and his black shoes had a brilliantly polished shine that reflected the ceiling lights. His hair remained unkempt as the man took off his military cap and placed it by his side revealing a full head of black hair, cut short, but yet long enough to reveal a natural wave to it.

"Mind if I join you for a cup of coffee? There is something I want to talk to you about," the Captain said as he sat down in the booth without being invited to do so. Josh was forced to move to the inside of the booth making room for the Captain to sit down.

"We're only staying for a few more minutes; we gotta' get back to the office." Josh informed Captain Bartholomew as he slid over in the booth.

"Good morning," the Sheriff offered, trying to be polite. He was uncomfortable with the interloper but gave him the same courtesy he would give anyone else. His first impression of the Captain was negative and he wasn't sure why.

Comfortable in his seat, the man reached into his shirt pocket, pulled out two business cards, and handed one to Josh and one to the Sheriff. Josh looked at it briefly until he noticed the name. He looked at it carefully this time wondering if there was a connection.

CAPTAIN JOHN PAUL BARTHOLOMEW II

UNITED STATES ARMY RESERVE OFFICER

U.S. ARMY RESERVE CENTER

335TH LIGHT EQUIPMENT SUPPORT ARMY

"You related to our pastor here in town?" Josh asked.

"Yes, he's my brother; I'm in town for a couple of weeks to spend some time with him," the Captain replied.

"How long have you been in the Reserve?" the Sheriff asked, trying to make conversation.

"Since I was in my early twenties, sir," the Captain answered as if the question was one of annoyance to him. "I don't have time to dilly-dally around this morning. How are you coming on these murder cases around here? A couple of weeks have gone by now and neither I nor anybody else in town really knows what the hell is going on. You must have some kind of evidence or clues or something by now."

The Sheriff was about to answer when the Captain continued. "I am here in this god-forsaken town to help my brother. He's having a hard time of it because the murder victims were all members of his church. I am here to try and help comfort him so the sooner we get this thing settled the sooner I can get the hell out of town."

Josh stared at the captain, surprised and confused by what he was hearing but more so, who it was coming from. "We've got several pieces of evidence, but we are not releasing anything right now. We don't want to jeopardize the case by leaking information that should not be known to the general public right now."

"In other words, you don't have shit," the Captain continued. "My brother's church has lost five of its members in the last few weeks and it hasn't been fun for him conducting funerals for such senseless deaths. I feel that I am very close to this case and I want some damned answers. You guys might start by checking who was attending the funerals. My brother says there is some guy that sits in the front row of the church and has been to all the funerals. I guess he just sits there and stares at my brother. He has never seen this guy before; he could be your killer. I know you have been recording the funerals so I know that you are aware of him."

"You're right; we've got him on video along with a lot of other people," Josh replied. "Maybe you can enlighten us a little. Is there anything about this case that you know about and we don't? Your brother knew all five of the victims, is there some kind of pattern or information that he could help us with?"

"I don't know anything more than you do. My brother said that none of them were regular church members and he was lucky to see them in church twice a year. He did talk a little about the Rawlings and the Anderson girls. He said that there was something strange about that relationship. Did you know that neither one of them ever had a boyfriend? Well, they didn't, and they kept to themselves and were always together. He knew that the Anderson girl had moved in with Rawlings. I think they were both queer and maybe there was some kind of love triangle going on."

The demeanor of the Captain was becoming more irritable to Josh but he allowed the Captain to speculate on the work they were doing with the case and the lives of the victims. He wanted to keep the Captain talking because he thought that there might be something here that was important to the investigation. "What did your brother think about the Helms' girl?"

"He didn't know her very well, but knew she divorced her husband after he gave her three children. Divorce is against God's will you know. After her divorce, she began seeing a lot of one of your deputies. Her life certainly wasn't exemplary. Maybe she was messing around with other men and one of them got jealous. Who knows, but I think there are a lot of suspects in this case and you guys better dig a little deeper into the backgrounds of the victims. You might find something," the Captain answered with a sarcasm that would imply that both Josh and the Sheriff were bungling idiots and handling the case more like Barney Fife than professional law enforcement people.

"You mentioned one of my deputies. I want to tell you that he is a very good man and that he and Mary Helms were talking of marriage, I wouldn't make something dirty out of that. Besides, I don't like anyone downgrading any of my men for no reason at all. That kind of talk could cause a lot of unnecessary rumors circulating around town," the Sheriff answered, looking directly into the glassy brown eyes of the Captain.

"Have it your way, Sheriff. I have to be going now." The Captain slid out of the booth and half saluted the two as they were still looking at the Captain in surprise and wonder.

The Captain walked toward the rear of the restaurant and out the back door. Josh pulled back the curtain from the window that was adjacent to their booth and looked out. He turned to the Sheriff, "he's getting into a half-track, can you beat that." He kept looking out the window and repeated himself one more time. "A half-track, can you beat that."

"Maybe he's afraid of getting stuck and wanted a big enough vehicle in case he did," the Sheriff replied.

"Hmmmm," Josh replied as he pulled another cigarette out of his pocket. "There is something wrong with that guy."

"Maybe he's one of those people that when they get a uniform on they think they are king shit," the Sheriff answered.

"It's more than that. I've dealt with a lot of people and this guy's got a screw loose." Josh said as if talking to himself and the Sheriff knew Josh's mind was once again spinning at a million miles an hour.

Milo looked at his watch, "I gotta' be going." He picked up the guest check lying in the middle of the booth. He slid out of the booth and walked toward the counter to pay the bill.

Josh followed and waited for the Sheriff at the front door. "Thanks for the coffee and roll. I'm going over to Odell's and see if I can have Tommy watch the video and see what kind of reaction I can get out of him."

"Okay, see you later," Milo said as he started walking toward his squad car.

As he drove toward the Graban home, he couldn't get the conversation with the Captain out of his mind. The Captain had given him an idea though, he would have to interview the members of the church, maybe there was more to all the victims being members of the same church. Josh decided to turn around and go back to the office; the Grabans would have to wait.

Josh got into the station and immediately called Amy Van Pre, the church secretary. He asked if he could stop by the church and pick up the latest copy of the church yearbook. She said she would have it waiting for him when he arrived. Thirty minutes later he had the yearbook and was on his way back to his office. The next two days were spent on the telephone calling as many church members as he could, trying to extract information on the murder victims.

Although most of the members knew Mary Helms and her children, they could shed no light on why they were murdered or if they had any enemies. None of them knew her well enough to have knowledge of her personal life and could offer very little information that would be of any help to Josh. When it came to the Rawlings girl and the Anderson girl, none of the members even knew who they were. They had heard rumors about the relationship between them, that they were possibly gay and were victims of some kind of love triangle, but that was all the help they could offer. The pastor was a favorite subject of most of the parishioners that Josh called. They were not used to him yet. He was so different from Pastor Crumb. Most of them seemed to like the pastor in a religious sense but few considered him a man who they could get close to. A lot of the members felt that *there was something about the man that made them uneasy* but *they couldn't lay their hands on it.* The only profile he had gotten from his telephone calls was that the pastor was always gone Tuesday nights and Wednesdays and no one seemed to know where he went. Other than that, everyone seemed somewhat satisfied with his performance as the pastor but he *wasn't as good as Pastor Crumb.*

Josh contacted the main Army Reserve Headquarters in St. Paul and talked to Colonel Riley. He had requested some information from the Reserves about Captain Bartholomew's career as an Army Reserve Officer. The Colonel told him that they would not release that kind of information but told Josh that the Captain had a distinguished career in the Reserves and was highly regarded as a leader and military man. He went on to say that there were no blemishes in his long career in the Reserves.

The last phone call of the day had been to Captain Bartholomew's commanding officer. Josh wondered if the day had been a complete loss and if Captain Bartholomew was worth investigating further. He would make that decision later; it was almost five thirty and he was getting tired. He went to the squad room for a smoke. He pulled out a cigarette and was about to light it when an impulse to visit his mother suddenly struck him. It should have struck him because he had promised his mother he would stop over for supper tonight and spend the evening with her. He finished his cigarette and hastily put it out; it would be his last one of the day. He was slowly weaning himself off cigarettes and was down to four a day.

He went back to his office and put on his winter coat and was about to shut the office door when he remembered that he needed to call Odell Graban and set up an appointment to view the video with Tommy. Odell invited him over the next evening for supper, told him to be there around five-thirty and they would eat at six. He was going to have some of the best home cooking in Bishop two nights in a row; he was looking forward to it.

- 13 -

The main street of Bishop was deserted with the exception of four cars parked in front of the Bishop municipal liquor store. The same cars were parked there each weekday night as a few of the local people stopped in for a drink before going home. For the most part, everyone in Bishop were in their homes by five thirty either eating or watching television or both. Most of the men and some of the women worked in nearby Cedarton where jobs were plentiful at Ace Manufacturing and wages above average.

The amber glow of the streetlights illuminated the small business district as Josh made his way past the stores toward the Grabans. He looked at his watch, it was five twenty. The nights were getting shorter as the street lights signaled that dusk was approaching. Main Street was blacktopped now but the stores were the same now as they were when he was growing up. Nothing had changed much in all those years. Change wasn't accepted well by the citizens of Bishop. The only new business was that of A & D Chevrolet, but that was out on the interstate. The first building on the block was Ace Manufacturing, which was the only vacant building on the block. The small company which produced power take-offs for tractors was suffering growing pains and made the decision to move to Cedarton where there was a more available work force to select from. Next was Harry's Grocery, a small store that sold everything from magazines to choice lobster tails. Harry's prices were higher than they should be but no one wanted to drive to Cedarton; it wasn't worth the time or the effort. Next to the grocery store was the pool hall, which had three pool tables and one snooker table; the owner charged two cents a minute for shooting pool and three cents a minute for snooker. The Pool Hall made good hamburgers and served beer in a frosted mug. An alley separated the barbershop, clothing store and implement store, which were all in one building owned by Nick Jones. Bill Johnson was finishing his window washing at the implement store while talking and gesturing to Nick. The town handyman and local philosopher glanced up at the sky and was happy he had finished his work before dusk. The two had to be discussing politics Josh thought to himself as he watch Bill's hands flaying and waving in the air as he always did when discussing his favorite.

On the other side of Main Street were the football field, a granary, and the Sheriff's Department. The grass on the field had recently turned light brown thanks to the recent frosts. The field was in good condition, tended to by the school custodians. The Cardinals hadn't had a winning season since he was on the team. Like most football players in the small school, he had to play both defensive and offensive positions. In his senior year, the Cardinals went undefeated thanks to its star running back Jackie Richmond who went on to captain the Minnesota Gophers, then turned pro and played for the Vikings for five seasons. He was killed in a car accident in St. Paul and the rumor was that he had been drinking.

Nonetheless, he was the local hometown hero and deserved recognition. The people of Bishop gathered a collection, erected a statue in his honor, and placed it at the entrance of the field next to the ticket booth.

Originally, the Sheriff's Department was a small brick building with an office and one single garage. There was a jail cell in the rear but rarely used. When Josh bought his first car, a 1949 black Ford with orange flames on the hood and fenders, he would cruise the main drag every Friday night with his friends. They would drive up and down the gravel street turning around at the creamery which was two blocks from the football field and then back up Main Street. Gas was twenty-nine cents a gallon and the whole night may cost him a dollar fifty in gas. Once in a while, they would chip their money together and buy a six-pack of beer, which would be split with him and his friends. Sheriff Bean always parked his squad car in the driveway of his office on Friday nights and stood outside of his car leaning on the hood and watched the cars cruise up and down. His presence kept everybody honest.

He made a left turn onto Pearl Street after passing the Bishop Cafe and made another left turn into the long narrow driveway that separated Graban Hardware from the Graban home. He stopped in front of the small, single car wooden garage and turned off his engine. The garage door had been pulled open and the Graban car was sitting in the garage with its hood up. Odell was leaning on the fender looking at the motor. Josh got out of his car and walked toward the garage as Odell lifted his head up from the engine and looked at Josh as he wiped his hands on a rag.

"Hi Josh, I'd shake your hand but mine are all full of grease. Got carburetor trouble and nobody seems to know how to work on those things properly."

"Good evening Odell, am I early?"

"Not a bit," Odell said as he closed the hood of the Chevrolet. "Just in time for a beer before we eat. Come inside while I wash up quick and we'll have a cold one."

"I'm going to get my stuff out of the car and I'll be right in." Josh said, then lit a cigarette and walked toward his car. When he finished his cigarette, he walked to the front door and knocked lightly.

"Just a minute," Betty Graban said as he heard her footsteps approaching. She opened the door and looked at Josh. "How are you Josh? Let me take your coat. Odell's getting you a beer."

He walked into the parlor where Odell was waiting with a beer in each hand. He took one and sat down in an overstuffed maroon mohair chair while Odell sat down on the edge of the matching couch.

The small talk switched from politics to football and then to the weather. He could smell the pleasant odor of the home cooked meal that was emanating from the kitchen. Betty Graban was recognized as one of the best cooks in Bishop and he was looking forward to the feast he was going to be treated to. He had been to his mother's last night for a big meal and now another one was about to be served to him. These were occasions he cherished because he would never make this kind of meal for himself. It was too much bother and there would be too many leftovers; he did not like leftovers. And besides that, he couldn't cook.

"Josh, if you want to set up your equipment now, go ahead. This is the room we're gonna' watch the videos in. Everything's all set up for it, all you gotta' do is put in the DVD." Odell said pointing to the DVD player on top of the TV.

Before he could answer, Betty informed Josh and Odell that supper was served. They got up from the parlor and brought their beers to the dining room table. The first thing Betty did was to dish up a plate of food for Tommy. Josh noticed that Tommy must have an appetite as she loaded his plate with mashed potatoes, squash, escalloped corn, and roast pork with a slice of homemade apple pie on a separate plate.

"This is for Tommy; he won't eat with us yet," Betty said.

"As you can see, Josh, he eats well but nothing else has changed." Odell remarked as he got up to take the plate of food upstairs to his grandson. When he returned to the table, Betty was waiting to say grace so they could begin eating.

"How're you and Marcie getting along with you working all the time?" Betty asked as a concerned mother would in talking to her son. "I know you are working hard on this case and we would all like to see it solved but a woman needs to have some attention paid to her."

"Things are fine, Betty. Marcie understands about the work I am doing and we do get together on weekends. She really is very understanding."

"How are you doing Betty? You're looking good." Josh asked.

"To tell you the truth, I really am feeling good. You know I was very depressed for a while over losing my daughter and grandchildren that way but I realized I had to put that in the past or I would end up in the nuthouse. Besides, I have other children and grandchildren to be with and a husband who needs my affections so I just don't allow myself any time to fret and worry about it. Even Odell here is getting better. I have never seen him take anything so hard in my life. He has been seeing a psychiatrist and the doctor thinks that after a few more visits, Odell will be back to the man he was before this all happened."

"Now dear, Josh doesn't want to hear about me," Odell said, blushing a little. "I do feel better though, Josh. I am going to open the store back up after the holidays. That is going to occupy my mind more and not allow me to think about the murders so much. I shouldn't tell you this, but I had even thought about suicide after I lost my daughter and grandchildren in that horrible way. I just couldn't figure anything out anymore and didn't want to live with that for the rest of my life."

"I am glad to hear that you both are doing better, I don't know how I'd handle it. It was a terrible thing. How about Tommy?"

"A little change, but not enough to get our hopes up. We've taken him to a lot of different specialists and have found one at the Mayo Clinic that we like. He's good and he feels that someday Tommy will come out of his shell. His name is Dr. Lebowitz and he's fairly young but he seems to know what he's doing. He said he would work with Tommy until he gets better. He seems to think that some kind of jolt to his mental faculties will break the hold this trauma has on him. That is why we have agreed to let him watch the video in hopes that something might be triggered that would help him get better. The only progression he has made so far is that he will now play with toys, which he wouldn't do before. He used to hide under his bed with a blanket over him, he would lie there all day and all night, and that was very frustrating for us to watch. He doesn't do that anymore and even moves around in his room now so we are getting our hopes up a little."

"Is he talking yet?" Josh asked.

"He hasn't uttered a sound since the incident with the TV and he won't eat with us. He eats only in his room with Squeaky." Odell answered.

Josh quickly demolished the plate of food that sat in front of him. Betty noticed his plate was empty. "Have some more food, there is plenty here," Betty said as she began passing second helpings around the table.

"Thanks," he said as he filled his plate for the second time, leaving room in his stomach for the homemade apple pie he knew was coming. After supper was finished, Betty cleared the table and carried the dirty plates, silverware, bowls, and cups to the kitchen.

"Why don't you two go into the parlor and have another beer, I'll be there shortly. It won't take me long, dishwashers are wonderful. Then we can go and get Tommy."

"Don't get Tommy just yet, I want to show the DVDs to you first and then talk a little before you bring him down," Josh said as he sat down in the mohair chair again. He watched Odell place a couple of oak logs in the fireplace. Lighting a newspaper, he placed it carefully under the logs and the dry wood instantly ignited emitting a blue and orange flame that instantly warmed up the parlor. The fireplace had been built with Chicago common brick, the mantle being made out of basswood and stained a chocolate brown. The pictures of the children and grandchildren were placed in a neat row on the mantle, all in gold framing. An 8 x 10 framed picture of Ben, Mary, Janet, Shara, and Tommy Helms stood erect in the center of the mantelpiece. Wainscoting surrounded the room with wallpaper covering the wall above it. It was comfortable and cozy and Josh thought to himself that he could easily grab a good book and read it in front of the fireplace and forget about the interview with Tommy. Betty came out of the kitchen wiping her hands on a light blue apron. She took off the apron, placed it on one of the dining room chairs, walked into the parlor, and sat down on the mohair couch next to her husband.

"I wanted you to see the DVD first and make a decision if you want Tommy to view them. I am not going to show him the first DVD of his mother's funeral; we've already gone through that. What

I am interested in knowing though is if he has a reaction while watching the second DVD. If he does, I think we can be fairly certain the murderer is in the church. I think he got a good look at the killer and is terrified of this person."

"Do you think the killer came to the funerals?" Odell asked, dismayed at the idea the murderer would find any joy in watching the suffering that takes place at a funeral.

"Yes, I do," Josh answered as he got up to put the first DVD in the machine. "This is from both the Rawlings' funeral and the Anderson funeral. I am going to point out a face that appears at both funerals. No one knows this guy, but he was at your daughter's funeral and these funerals. I am going to point him out to you and I want you to study him. So far, no one has recognized him and I am hoping you might." Odell and Betty watched the DVD of the Rawlings funeral and the Anderson funeral. When the stranger appeared, Josh put the DVD on stop-action for the Grabans to study. They looked at the picture carefully but said that they had never seen the man before now. "I was hoping differently, you know," Josh said. "That done, do you think Tommy should see these?"

Betty and Odell sat on the couch looking at each other for some sign of reassurance that this wouldn't affect Tommy. After a few minutes of silence, Odell got up. "What have we got to lose," Odell said and walked toward the stairs to get his grandson. Odell walked down the stairs with his hand in Tommy's. The boy, who at his age should have been bouncing and leaping down the staircase, was walking slowly as if he was being taken out to the woodshed for a spanking. His eyes were hollow and his small mouth twisted downwards silently expressing deep sadness. He walked with Odell into the parlor and sat down in front of the TV. Squeaky followed and jumped onto his lap.

Josh put the disk of the Rawlings' funeral into the DVD player and turned it on. Tommy watched for two or three minutes and then tears began running down both cheeks. Without a sound he got up, walked over to the television, and began pounding on the screen. Squeaky began barking and running around the parlor in small circles stopping at the TV after each loop, barking directly at the screen. Odell got up from the couch, picked Tommy up and took him back to his room with Squeaky following close behind.

"Maybe that wasn't such a good idea. I better call Dr. Lebowitz," Betty said as she got up and went to the phone and dialed his number. "Hello, Dr. Lebowitz" she began and then explained what had happened. "Five milligrams, okay, we'll bring him over tomorrow, thank you, doctor."

When Odell came back downstairs, Josh got up and apologized for what happened. "After watching both Tommy's and Squeaky's reaction I feel certain they recognized the murderer somewhere in that church. All I got to do now is figure out who it is. I am going to pursue this as hard as I can, don't worry, we'll catch this guy."

"It wasn't your fault, Josh, we want to find the killer as bad as you do. Don't worry, Dr. Lebowitz didn't seem to think any harm was done," Betty said and offered Josh another beer.

"No thanks, I should be going. Thanks for the wonderful meal and your cooperation in this whole thing," Josh answered putting the DVD's in his briefcase while Betty went to the closet, retrieved his coat, and brought it to him.

He opted to stop at Pete's for a beer before going home. He didn't have to prepare supper tonight so had a little extra time to kill. Walking in the front door, he noticed Marcie sitting at a small table with two of the girls from her office. She looks lovely tonight he thought to himself as he walked over to the table. Noticing him, Marcie look surprised. She smiled and pointed to an empty chair at their table. "Have a seat." He sat down and joined the conversation. He was having a good time and the time was going by fast. He was enjoying Marcie's friends but after two beers, he glanced at his watch and realized it was time to go. Tomorrow might be a very busy and productive day and he needed a good night's sleep.

- 14 -

A cloud of caution and nervousness loomed over the town and wouldn't be lifted until the killer was found. It was a week before Christmas and the citizens of Bishop were in a solemn mood. No one left their doors unlocked and several houses had alarm systems installed. Gun stores in Cedarton were doing a booming business; the people of Bishop were arming themselves. Wives accompanied their husbands and husbands accompanied wives; no one stayed home alone anymore.

With Christmas approaching the town was relaxing a little. The murders were still on the minds of everyone but the holiday season had a way of making you forget your troubles. This year was no different and as Christmas approached the normal holiday activities resumed. Instead of being a busy time of year for the Sheriff's Department, it was one of the quietest holidays that Sheriff Milo Bean could remember. The Sheriff desperately needed some time off so he and his wife flew to Las Vegas for a short three-day vacation. He left Frank Blume in charge of the department in his absence, beginning the preparations for grooming him to be the next Sheriff. Josh had turned his offer down and he was comfortable with Frank.

Winter viciously attacked southern Minnesota on Halloween night but the weather eventually calmed and turned mild. Since the Halloween storm another six inches of snow had sporadically fallen but most of it had disappeared. A few splotches could be spotted in shaded areas but the sun had done a good job of melting most of it. A few of the farmers had not picked their crops when the storm hit. But most of the farmers had and were in a good mood. Their crops were out and prices were good, for both corn and soybeans. Year after year, the crop farmer worried whether he would be able to get his field planted; the weather was always the deciding factor. He needed a dry spring, a wet but hot summer, and a dry fall to get the optimum yield on his crops. The weather never cooperated ideally for him so the farmer was always in a constant state of angst over his crops. Most of the farmers did not raise cattle or hogs to supplement their income but relied solely on their crops to provide a decent living. This year had been good for the farmer; when the farmer made money, so did the town's businesses.

The Bishop Cafe was having a good few months in sales also. The wives were insisting they go with their husbands to the coffee shop; they were not going to stay home alone with a killer loose. The men weren't too excited about this arrangement but they all eventually relented and brought their wives with them to the morning coffee routine. The conversation took on a new tone; the talk of politics had been replaced with discussions about grandchildren and the exchanging of recipes. Something had to be done and done quickly; the men were tired of having their privacy broken and were somewhat perplexed as how to handle the problem. They couldn't tell their wives they did not wish to talk about recipes and grandchildren. They wanted 'man talk' to return and yearned to discuss politics, sports, and the economy like in the 'good old days'. If they got the wives mad though they would have to stay home and miss out on the most important time of their day. The men were suffering a dilemma.

One day, Bill Johnson had a brilliant idea but did not tell anyone about it except Dolly. He gave her twenty dollars and asked her to buy a flower arrangement and set it on table three. She was to place an envelope on the bouquet which said "Girls Table". Table three was usually empty at that time of the morning and he hoped his plan would work. The next morning, Mrs. Didier came into the restaurant with her husband and noticed the bouquet and the card on the flowers. She sat there and was soon joined by the other wives as they came in. From that morning on, the wives had their own table and were happy and the men now had their table and privacy back. Things were once again back to normal at the Bishop Cafe.

Josh and Marcie began seeing more of each other. The murder case had come to a standstill and Josh had more time for Marcie. He was tired of dating several women and wanted to settle down with Marcie. He enjoyed her and wanted a deeper relationship with her. They were seen together most of the time now and had become a 'hot' item in Bishop. He had thought about asking Marcie to move in with him but he still enjoyed his privacy too much. Marriage had more than once entered their conversations but Josh was a very private person and he wasn't sure if it would work. He would think about it some more. He would weigh the pros and the cons of marriage and sharing the rest of his with life Marcie. He just couldn't make up his mind.

Tom Jenks was obsessed about finding the killer. He had been in love with Mary Helms and felt cheated that her life was taken from him. He could have had a lifetime of happiness with her, he thought, and he felt a void in his life he believed could never be filled by another woman. He pursued all leads relentlessly, going over them again and again in hopes of finding one little piece of evidence that might break the case wide open. He spent all of his waking hours thinking about the case, thinking of nothing else. He returned to the murder scenes several times looking for something that might have been missed. He wanted desperately for Tommy to regain his mental health and be able to reveal who the murderer was. This might not happen for a long time, but he had the patience to wait. Tom was convinced the stranger in the church held the key to this whole mystery.

The Graban family had rented a cabin in northern Minnesota and decided that they would get out of Bishop and celebrate the holidays with their family in a more secluded area. Tommy was going along with the family even though he hadn't shown much progress. The family had gotten used to taking care of him and felt comfortable with his presence.

Frank Blume was overwhelmed when Sheriff Bean called him into his office and offered him the same opportunity he had offered Josh earlier. He told Frank of his plans to retire and why. Frank was surprised but seemed to understand. The Sheriff told Frank he would become more involved in the day-to-day operations of the department. When Sheriff Bean felt Frank was ready to run the department, he would retire and hand over the reins of the department to him. This way he would have a couple years of experience as Sheriff before the elections and should win his first election easily. The Sheriff told Frank he would endorse him for election but didn't think there would be any opposition.

On Christmas Eve, the Abundant Life Church held a candlelight vigil for the twenty-eight people who had been killed in the storm and for the five murder victims. It seemed like Davis County had been hard hit with tragedies the past year and the church wanted to do something special. Deputy Jenks attended the vigil hoping the stranger would appear. Pastor Bartholomew led the congregation in the solemn service.

Almost everyone in town attended the memorial service and the candlelight vigil. The pews were filled to capacity with mourners, relatives, and curiosity seekers. Crowds of people stood in the rear of the church while others camped on the lawn outside the church. Deputy Jenks was busy scanning the faces of all in attendance but he did not see the man he had been looking for. Pastor Bartholomew delivered a short homily attempting to make sense out of the senseless tragedies of the last year. He was distraught as he spoke, fumbling with his words while trying to reassure the people of Bishop that better times were ahead. The vigil lasted until four in the morning with the Grabans being the last to leave. They immediately left town and returned to their cabin. At first, they weren't going to attend the vigil, but at the last minute changed their minds and drove the two hundred miles to attend the service. Pastor Bartholomew had a six o'clock sunrise service to lead in a couple of hours. He decided it would be best if he did not sleep so he studied his sermon in his office and dozed off and on. The two later services would be conducted by the intern and he could then go home to sleep. The day after Christmas was Tuesday and he would leave for Minneapolis.

- 15 -

It was midway between Christmas and New Years when the dispatcher at the Sheriff's department received a phone call from the daughter of Mattie Blake.

"This is Sandy Thompson. I'm not at my home in Bishop right now, I'm out of town, and I need your help."

The caller didn't seem nervous or upset which was a great help to the dispatcher. It was very difficult at times to get the correct information from a hysterical caller. The dispatcher went to her computer, ready to key in the information she was about to receive from the caller. "Could you please give me your address?"

"922 Locust Avenue, in Bishop."

"What is your phone number?"

"I'm going to give you my cell phone number; we don't have a land line anymore." She repeated the number twice, wanting to make sure the dispatcher copied it down correctly.

"Okay, what can we do for you?"

"Well, I haven't heard from my mother since Christmas and she usually calls me at least once a day to check in with me and also to let me know how she is doing. If she doesn't call, I call her. I called her again today and there was still no answer and she hasn't contacted me at all, I'm beginning to get worried. This has never happened before and I thought maybe you could check on her for me."

"Maybe she has been visiting someone or gone out of town for a while," the dispatcher answered, hoping put her mind at ease.

"I know I told you that I hadn't heard from her since Christmas but that's wrong. Our family is spending the holidays with my husband's relatives in Wisconsin so I really have not heard from her since Saturday. I thought maybe I had missed her calls so I keep checking my messages. There were none. She always leaves a message if I don't answer. I hope nothing is wrong and I will feel better after someone checks the house."

"So, you are still in Wisconsin."

"Yes, we won't be home until after New Year's."

"Why don't you give me your mother's address and I will send a squad car out to her house to see if everything is all right."

"Okay, she lives about five miles south of Cedarton on county road 35. As you are heading south, it is on the right hand side. It is a two story yellow house with a double car garage. It is the only yellow house in the area so it shouldn't be too hard to find.

If she's home there will be a black four-door Honda parked in the driveway."

The dispatcher wrote down the information from the caller that she needed and told Sandy Thompson that she would call after the deputies checked on her mother. After she got off the phone, she called the patrol deputy in the Cedarton area and asked that he stop and check on the welfare of one Mattie Blake.

Deputy Bones Crawford was sitting in a booth at McDonalds enjoying a large breakfast when he received the call from the dispatcher. The call was not an emergency so he finished his breakfast before heading out of Cedarton to check on Mattie Blake. He knew the location of the house; he had driven by it many times.

Two years ago, Arnold Crawford joined the Sheriff's department. The deputies christened him with the nickname of 'Bones' because of his tall, lean, and lanky appearance. He was six feet five inches tall with only a one hundred and fifty pound frame to go with it. He could run like a gazelle and never lost a prisoner who made the mistake of trying to outrun him. As Bones drove toward the Blake home, he could not help but notice the isolation that went with living in the country. It was cold outside and Bones was wearing winter underwear, heavy wool pants, a thick leather vest, a parka, and a fuzzy winter cap and was still cold. The heater in the squad car kept him warm but when he got out of the car he was prepared for the cold blast that would hit him. Driving down the county road, he noticed there was very little snow cover on the ground; the rich black soil in the fields was frozen solid. The trees had shed their leaves for the winter so the beautiful color of green did not exist anywhere. He longed to live someplace warm and green year round. Maybe it was because of his lack of body fat that he was cold all the time. He could never get warm, except for some of the hot, humid days of July. The summers were always too short and he dreaded winter more each coming year.

The two-tone brown squad car pulled up the driveway and parked in back of the black Honda. Bones got out of the squad car and studied the yard. Seeing nothing, he walked toward the back entryway. He pulled open the screen door, rapped on the inside door and waited for an answer. Not getting it, he walked to the front of the house and walked up some steps that led to a large porch. Walking along the porch, he looked into two large windows, hoping to see Mattie. Not seeing any signs of her he knocked on the front door. Mattie had to be home, her car was here, he thought to himself. When she didn't come to the front door, he began yelling Mattie's name but there was only silence. After failing to get her attention, he reached for the doorknob and turned it; it was locked. He returned to the rear door and tried to turn the knob, the door was unlocked; Deputy Crawford pushed it partly open and yelled Mattie Blake's name. Not getting a response, he opened the door further and walked into the kitchen. He yelled Mattie's name several times. Getting no answer, he was beginning to worry that something might be terribly wrong with Mattie. He cautiously checked the dining room, the living room, master bathroom, and downstairs bathroom. Everything appeared to be in its place so he climbed the stairs to the second floor. The second floor contained three small bedrooms, two large closets, and a bathroom. He checked the bedrooms first, then the closets. Still seeing nothing out of the ordinary, he walked toward the bathroom and slowly pushed open the slightly ajar bathroom door. Mattie was lying on the floor in a fetal position, a pool of blood under her head. He knelt down and put his hand on Mattie's neck, hoping for a pulse; there was none. Rigor mortis was developing; Mattie had been dead for a while. He left her as she was, pulled his portable Motorola radio from his gun belt, and called the Law Enforcement Center. The dispatcher answered his radio call and Bones asked to speak to the Sheriff.

"Go ahead."

"Sheriff, I'm at Mattie Blake's. I think you better come out here and bring Josh along. Dooble's been at work again."

"I'll get there as soon as I can. Josh isn't here so I have got to round him up first. Hope to be there in less that an hour. Hold down the fort until I get there."

The Sheriff found Special Agent Trimble at Marcie's and told him about his conversation with Deputy Crawford. Sheriff Bean parked his unmarked dark blue unmarked squad car in front of Marcie's and waited. He didn't have to wait long; in a couple of minutes, Josh opened the front door and set two metal suitcases on the steps. The Sheriff got out of his squad and walked up to Josh. "Need a hand with that stuff?"

"Thanks, I got another suitcase in the house. If you could carry these two out to the car, it would be a big help."

The Sheriff helped Josh put the two suitcases filled with lab equipment on the rear seat. When Josh returned from the apartment with his third suitcase, he got into the front seat of the squad car and put the suitcase on the floor in front of him. Satisfied they had everything they needed he pulled his squad car from the curb and drove toward the County shop. Waiting for Josh to bring out his equipment, he noticed that he was low on gas. It was a good half hour drive to Mattie Blake's and he didn't want to run out of gas; he would never hear the end of it from his deputies. The Sheriff stopped at the County gas pumps, filled the squad car, and headed for Mattie Blake's.

Bones was busy putting up the familiar yellow crime scene tape around the house when the Sheriff's squad car pulled into the driveway and parked behind his squad car. The Sheriff and Josh walked up to Bones as he was finishing up with the tape.

"What ya' got?"

"Got a call from dispatch to check on Mattie Blake. Her daughter hadn't heard from her for a couple of days and I guess she was worried. Came out from Cedarton and parked next to her car. Thought as long as her car was there, she must be home. Knocked on the door and got no answer. Back door was open so I walked in and yelled her name. Found her lying on the bathroom floor upstairs. She's been dead for a while; rigor mortis is already setting in. Throat's been cut."

The Sheriff and Josh entered the house through the partially ajar back door. They explored the first floor carefully walking from room to room looking for any evidence of a struggle or anything amiss. Everything appeared normal and in their place on the main floor. Satisfied with their search so far they ascended the staircase and carefully examined three bedrooms on the second floor before walking to the murder scene. The bathroom door was open. Josh was the first to enter the small bathroom and his eyes immediately went to the floor of the bathroom where Mattie Blake lay in a pool of thick semi-hardened blood. Josh took out his cell phone and called the crime scene investigators telling them what he had and that he needed a unit at the scene. Closing his cell phone, he informed the Sheriff that it would be a couple of hours before they would be able to get here. Looking around the bathroom, he spied the expected calling card sitting on top of the toilet. Josh carefully picked it up by its corners and looked at it wondering what the next letter stood for. He held it up and showed it to the Sheriff 'DEATH. ON. OTHERS. BY. LIVING. E'. He laid it back on the toilet tank top; the crime guys would bag it later. Glancing at the body of Mattie Blake, Josh noticed the victim's hair had been hastily lopped off; the killer was getting sloppier or he was in a hurry for some reason. There was no jewelry on the victim except a thin gold wedding band. It appeared as if the killer tried to get the ring off but had no luck. The wedding ring finger was badly bruised or possibly broken. Josh wondered why the killer would go to all the trouble of trying to remove the ring and then leave it. Maybe something spooked him, but what? The victim was fully clothed and it appeared there had not been a rape or attempted rape; the pathologist would determine that.

Josh had gotten all the information he needed. He walked out of the bathroom with the Sheriff close behind; they descended the stairs and walked outside where Josh lit up a cigarette and studied the exterior of the house and the yard. After he finished his cigarette, he told the Sheriff he could call the coroner.

Prior to the murder of Mattie Blake, the weather had been acting very strangely. One day the temperature would rise to forty–five or fifty degrees; the next day the thermometer would hover around zero. The thawing and the freezing caused the soil to soften from the warmth and then harden as the temperature dropped. A set of tire tracks had been left on the gravel driveway next to Mattie's black Honda. The tracks matched the tracks left at the other scenes and an imprint of a sandal near the tire tracks convinced Josh that the killer parked his car in the driveway and entered the house through the rear door. Josh wondered if Mattie had known her killer and willingly let him in the house. He was beginning to wonder if all the victims knew their killer. It was certainly a possibility.

If it was the killer's car, the crime lab could narrow the time of death within a couple of hours by comparing the tracks and the temperature variations in the last thirty-six hours. Josh was sure the evidence would prove the same person was responsible for all the murders, confirming what the dooble team already knew.

The Sheriff was wondering where he would find the manpower to station yet another deputy at another crime scene. He had a list of part-time deputies he could use and he might have to do just that. He couldn't afford to use another full time deputy; someone had to protect the County. The crime scene needed to be protected from curious sightseers who would be descending on the house and yard as soon as word was released to the media about another murder.

The Sheriff's job was done at Mattie Blake's. He radioed dispatch and informed her that he was returning to the office. The dispatcher relayed to the Sheriff that the local radio station was trying contact him in regard to the recent murder. He told the dispatcher to tell them he would call them back when he returned to the office. He didn't have much to tell them yet but he could feel the pressure mounting to solve the case, and soon. He was physically exhausted and his deputies, Bones, Frank Blume, and Tom Jenks were feeling the affects of not enough sleep and long hours of work. Hanging up the mike after talking to the dispatcher an idea came to him. He called his deputies and offered to buy them supper at the Bishop Cafe if they could be there in thirty minutes. No one refused his offer and they all arrived at the Cafe within fifteen minutes of the Sheriff.

The deputies joined their boss at a table near the back of the restaurant. They ordered coffee and looked at the menus that lay in front of them.

"Anybody know what the special is?" Frank asked as he studied his menu.

"Turkey and dressing," replied Bones. "They also got lemon meringue pie."

They all ordered the special and none of them ordered dessert except Bones.

"How'n the hell can you eat so much, Bones?" the Sheriff asked, always astounded at the amount of food that his skinniest deputy could devour at one sitting. "Where do you put it all?"

Bones chuckled. He was constantly eating but never put on any weight. He wanted to add twenty pounds to his weight; it would offer some insulation on the cold days but no matter how hard he tried, his weight remained the same.

"Where's Dolly tonight?" the Sheriff asked the young waitress.

"She's bowling. Their team is in first place and she's their best bowler, ya' know." She answered, chewing a large wad of gum. "She won't miss a game, the team won't let her."

After the waitress left, the Sheriff, looking and acting tired and frustrated, reviewed the events of the day. It had become all too familiar to him and his deputies by now. "The modus operandi's the same in each murder so we've got ourselves a serial killer loose in our county and I want him caught and I want him caught bad. That would be the best retirement present you could give me. And you know what is even worse, I think we all know the killer and he lives right here in Bishop. It's a gut feeling but I am usually right in these things."

Josh showed up at the restaurant late, sat down and waited for the waitress to appear and take his order. He caught the last part of the Sheriff's statement and added. "I'm certain those tire tracks we found belong to the killer and that partial footprint will be a match to the prints we found at the Helms murders. If it is the same as the one found at the Helms murders and I am sure it will be we can be certain the same person killed Mattie. The killer entered Mattie's house through the back door. There were no signs of forced entry so I am thinking that Mattie knew who the person was and willingly let him into the house. Of course, she might have accidently left the back door unlocked but I don't think so. The front door was locked and dead bolted which tells me that Mattie Blake was security conscious. We need to find out who was known by all the victims, it's going to be a monumental task but I think we're up to it."

"What kind of guy wears sandals in the winter?" Bones asked.

"Who knows, I have no idea of who we are dealing with here. Yea, this guy is something else, Bones," Josh answered.

"I called the hospital for you, Sheriff." Frank interrupted. "They have scheduled an autopsy for ten o'clock tomorrow morning."

"I'll be there." Josh told Frank and then asked the Sheriff if he wanted to go along.

"No need. In fact I've got a news conference with the Twin Cities papers tomorrow morning. I guess they're going ahead with a story on all the murders here. I don't relish talking to 'em but its all part of the job."

"Lucky you," Tom Jenks commented.

"I'll give 'em what we got which ain't much. Tell 'em we think the murders were committed by the same person and we are gathering more evidence which we hope will lead us to the killer soon, very soon. I'll tell them we don't have enough for an arrest yet and to be patient, we are trying our best." The Sheriff turned to Frank, "Remember, we give them as few details as we can get but enough so they don't crucify us in the paper."

Everyone was done eating and patiently waiting for Bones to finish his last bite of pie. The deputies and Josh thanked the Sheriff for the meal.

"I'm going to call it a night and I'll see you all in the morning," Milo said as he got up from his chair and walked to the counter to pay the bill. The same waitress that waited on his group was the same one at the register and he thanked her for the good service and left a generous tip. Walking to his car he could think only of a nice warm comfortable bed to sleep in; he was worn out and retirement couldn't come soon enough.

Josh looked at his watch, it was still early. Marcie had called and told him she was going to be at Pete's and wondered if he would like to join her. He told her he would be there but wasn't sure when. Looking at his watch, he realized he would be able to meet Marcie earlier than he planned. Marcie, like the other ladies of Bishop, did not wish to be home alone until the killer was caught. She was sitting at a small round table with two dispatchers from the law enforcement center when Josh walked in. A near empty pitcher of beer was sitting in the middle of the table, a pile of pull-tabs were scattered around it and some had spilled onto the floor. Josh spotted Marcie immediately and walked over to the table. An empty chair was waiting for him and he sat down before realizing that another pitcher of beer was needed. There was an empty glass on the table and Josh poured the rest of the pitcher into it. "Win anything?" he asked as he pulled out a five-dollar bill to buy some pull-tabs for himself.

"Yea, we're each about twenty bucks up, but you wouldn't think so by the pile in front of us. We decided to pocket the winnings and quit while we're ahead," one of the dispatchers answered. "Mattie Blake got murdered, huh?" the dispatcher continued. "Any luck on this one?"

"No, all we know is that it was done by the same person."

"She was really a nice person. I got to know her through our church. She was quite involved in the church and donated a lot of her time. I think she was mainly involved in the kitchen though," the other dispatcher offered.

"What church was that?" Josh asked.

"Is there any other church in town? Abundant Life, of course."

"Does everybody in town go to that church?" Josh curiously asked. The coincidences were starting to pile up. All the victims belonged to the same church; all the victims were female; and all the murders were happening just before or around a holiday. *There was something else, but what was it?* he thought to himself.

"No, but about half the town does. It's always been that way. We've had several churches try to start up but they never succeeded. People here are kind of set in their ways and don't like a lot of change. Well, these new start-up churches couldn't get anybody to even try them so they left as fast as they came. Word must be out because we haven't had one try for a couple of years now," the other dispatcher added.

Josh got up, walked to the bar, and ordered another pitcher of beer and five dollars worth of pull-tabs.

"How's it going, Pete?"

"Hey, Josh," Pete answered as he was filling the pitcher of beer that Josh had just ordered. "It's going pretty good considering everyone is pretty edgy right now. How you coming on those murder cases?"

"We're getting close, Pete. Real close, but not enough to make an arrest yet," Josh lied, but it was all he could think to say at the moment. He wanted to give some glimmer of hope that something was coming together. He would feel stupid saying he really didn't have much after six murders. "Thanks for the beer. Here, keep the change," he said as he began carrying the beer back to the table.

They drank two more pitchers of beer and ended up closing the bar which was unusual for both Marcie and Josh. They knew they would suffer for it in the morning. Josh had to meet with the pathologist at ten and so could sleep in but Marcie had to be at work at seven and he knew she would have a long day. He knew they would cool it tomorrow night.

Josh was at the hospital at quarter to ten waiting for the pathologist. He knew his friend would be late. He was late for everything and Josh jokingly told him once that he would be late for his own funeral. Josh knew the pathologist well and counted him as one of his best friends. His name was William Stolichinsky but everyone called him "Stoly" because no one could pronounce his name right. In this community, everyone seemed to have a nickname.

Stoly was about the same age as his friend Josh. He was short in stature and wore a neatly trimmed gray beard that did not correspond with his balding, disheveled hair. His reading glasses, which he wore at all times, rested on the tip of his nose and the lenses were usually smudged. Josh could never understand how he could see through them. Stoly was about twenty pounds overweight and dressed sloppily, usually wearing wrinkled black jeans and a white dress shirt that he sometimes forgot to button completely. He appeared absent-minded at times but Josh respected his ability and thought he was the best pathologist in the State. Stoly liked his beer and could drink Josh under the table but never seemed to get drunk. They had done many things together. They had attended Twins and Vikings games, followed the Gophers, and went on any of the available bus trips to see a game. Since Josh met Marcie, he and Stoly hadn't seen as much of each other. Stoly rarely spent time with his wife and hardly mentioned her. In fact, Josh had met his wife only once. She seemed nice enough but very quiet, just the opposite of Stoly. At ten fifteen, Stoly appeared, extended his hand to Josh, and said 'good morning'.

"You look a little pale today my friend. Have too much to drink last night?"

"Yea, Yea, Yea, let's get to work," Josh answered, trying to avoid the subject of last night. Stoly wouldn't let up and badgered Josh during the entire autopsy.

The autopsy didn't reveal any more than the previous ones. The time of death was determined to be the Saturday evening before Christmas and death was instantaneous. The fingernails were clean with no evidence of rape or semen anywhere on the body. The knife used was similar or the same one used in the other murders. It was a large knife, possible a Bowie style and extremely sharp.

"Sorry, we didn't find more, Josh, but something will turn up. Trust me, it always does." The reassurance by Stoly didn't help. He had rarely been in this situation and he didn't like it.

Two days after the murder of Mattie Blake, Amy Van Pre, always the prompt one, arrived at her desk at eight a.m. sharp. She laid her purse down, turned on the office lights, the copier, and lastly her computer. She opened her purse, took out a small key and unlocked her desk drawer, and methodically replaced the key back into her purse. She walked into the pastor's office to see if he was working and noticed him kneeling on the floor under his desk. The Pastor was caught by surprise and bumped his head on the bottom of the desk as he tried to extricate himself from the position he was in. He hastily put a small piece of paper in his shirt pocket, hoping Mrs. Van Pre had not noticed.

"Another burglary?" she asked, looking around the office and noticing the books from the bookcase had been strewn all over the floor. The drawers of his desk had been pulled out and the contents strewn about. "This is the third one so far. Don't you think we should call the police?"

"No, Mrs. Van Pre. I'll eventually find out who it is and I will have a talk with him. We don't want to drag the police into this. They have more important things to do."

"Was any thing taken?" Mrs. Van Pre asked, angry that such a mess had to once again be cleaned up.

"I can't see that anything is missing. I don't know what he has been looking for. I will do this though. If it happens again, maybe I will call the police. You're probably right, but let's hold off a while, okay?"

"You know," Mrs. Van Pre stated, as if something had clicked in her mind. "Each burglary happened just after those murders. That's right. After the Helms murder, we had a burglary. After the Rawlings and Anderson murders, we had a burglary. And now Mattie Blake. Maybe there's a connection, Pastor. We should call the police."

"No, not yet," he said, glaring at her to let her know that he was serious about this and he did not want her meddling into his affairs and that he would take care of it.

- 16 -

Deputy Jenks arrived at the church an hour before the funeral. The somber black Lincoln hearse sat idling under the large overhang that covered the front entrance to the church. Behind the hearse was the Pastor's car followed by family vehicles. The large concrete parking lot was empty; he parked in the rear of the lot next to a dumpster and surreptitiously waited for the mourners to arrive. From his vantage point, he was able to watch everyone who entered the church. He would know if the stranger was there. He wasn't going to film the funeral today; he was only there to look for the stranger. He was going to sit in the front pew on the left side of the church and study the stranger, if he showed up, and Tom Jenks was certain he would. A few minutes before the service was to begin the stranger still had not appeared so he go out of his squad car and entered the church through the kitchen door and walked into the church's nave. He stood there for a minute, scanning its interior hoping to see the stranger. Noticing the front pew on the left side was empty, he walked to it and sat down. He was in plain clothes, wearing a brown and dated suit with a faded yellow shirt and dark blue tie. He couldn't remember the last time he wore that suit. It didn't fit as well as it did when he first bought it and he felt a little uncomfortable wearing it.

Tom sat in the pew alone, nervous and disappointed, wondering if he had misjudged the stranger. He stared at the pulpit, then the cross, then the pulpit again. His mind an abyss, thinking of nothing. He had been sitting a couple of minutes when the stranger suddenly appeared and sat down in next to him. Tom turned to the stranger and gestured a brief nod; the stranger returned the acknowledgment. This man was a killer, he knew it. He must keep his senses about him and not alert the man in any way. Attempting to form a mental picture of the man, he committed to memory, as best he could the man's complexion and his facial features. The man sitting next to him was definitely Hispanic. His black hair was thick and wavy, overly greased but combed neatly back, almost touching his collar. A small diamond earring was clearly visible in his left ear. He was clean-shaven and neatly dressed. He did not look like a killer, but again, what did a killer look like. As a rookie, he could only guess. The stranger had a cheerless face with deep wrinkles on his forehead and pronounced crows feet at the corners of his eyes. It was the face of a man who had endured a lot of pain or sadness. He looked to be about thirty-five, but his face revealed a different story.

The church was filling up and the ushers were hurriedly setting up folding chairs to accommodate everyone. Mattie had truly been one of the church's most ardent volunteers and had earned the love and respect of the parishioners and the townspeople. The pallbearers brought the casket down to the front of the church and took their seat on the right side of the church. Pastor Bartholomew gave a brief sermon about Mattie and her work in the church. He went on to talk about her children and grandchildren and that she had surely lived a Godly life. He continued his eulogy by talking about the tragedies of the past and that we should all pray to God that this person be caught so there would be no more funerals at Abundant Life Church for a long time. The funeral lasted a little over twenty minutes. When it was over the pallbearers rose in unison and wheeled the casket out of the church and to the waiting hearse. The family members, most of them crying, followed behind the casket. The visitors then arose from their pews and followed the procession out of the church. This was Tom's chance to slip behind the stranger and follow him. After leaving the church, the stranger walked immediately to his vehicle, got in, and drove off. Tom was parked only a few stalls away. He got in his car and radioed dispatch that he was back in service and would be following a newer model Ford Tempo. He gave the dispatcher the license number of the car and asked for a license check.

In an instant, he received a radio call from the dispatcher informing him that the vehicle was owned by Budget Rent-a-Car and had been rented from the Minneapolis airport. Tom continued following the car in his unmarked vehicle on the freeway that led to Cedarton. The driver was cautious, carefully obeying all traffic laws and Tom guessed he knew he was being followed. He stayed behind the Tempo past Cedarton where it continued north. He must be going to Minneapolis he thought as he noticed the highway sign informing him he was at the County line. He was no longer in his jurisdiction. Using a turnaround, he entered the other side of the freeway and returned to Bishop.

Entering the church parking lot, he pulled his squad car into the same parking stall he had used before. He looked forward to attending the traditional luncheon that customarily followed a funeral service. He walked to the social hall and peered in the door. He was in time; the line was just beginning to form. A feast of major proportions was being served by the women of the church. Ham, chicken, hot dish, scalloped potatoes, corn, dinner rolls, and an assortment of pies were on the tables, waiting to be scooped up by the friends of Mattie Blake. Tom Jenks got in line and filled his plate with homemade hot dish and an assortment of salads and a piece of apple pie. He set his plate down at one of the long tables and walked over to offer his condolences to the family. He knew he would be asked several questions about the investigation and was prepared to answer them as best he could in hopes of stopping any rumors before they got started. Many questions were asked and he answered them as best as he could. It was evident the citizens of Bishop were worried and anxious but he couldn't find the words to ease their concerns. Tom stayed at the luncheon for over an hour and left, wondering if he had said too much.

Upon leaving the church, Deputy Jenks drove to the Law Enforcement Center, called the Budget Rent-a-Car office at the Minneapolis airport, and asked for information on the rental car driven by the stranger. The clerk was friendly and pleasant but told the deputy she couldn't release any information without some form of ID. She suggested he come to their office and talk to the station manager. The manager was the only one that could give him that information and one was available 24/7.

Hanging up the phone Tom knew what he needed to do but first had to get permission from the Sheriff. He went to his office but it was empty so he hurriedly walked to the dispatch center and called him on the radio.

"Go ahead, Tom," the Sheriff answered.

"Can you give me a call at the office? It's kind of important," Tom replied.

The Sheriff called immediately on his cell phone and Tom explained about the stranger being at the funeral and that he followed him north on I-35 but lost him at the County line. He explained that he called the Budget office at the airport and that they needed him to come in person and present some identification before they would release any information. He gave the Sheriff a brief description of the stranger and told him about the car. He asked his permission to let him drive to Minneapolis to the Budget office and find out who had rented the vehicle. Milo gave his consent and Tom anxiously got in his squad car, checked the gas and noticing that the tank was almost full began the one hour drive to the Minneapolis airport.

He easily found the airport and drove down the long entrance road to the parking ramps. He had never been to the airport and was astonished when he found out he had to pay ten dollars to park his vehicle for only a few minutes. It was highway robbery. He knew he would get reimbursed for the cost but he thought the fee was exorbitant. The girl at the Budget counter asked him for some kind of identification even though he was wearing the familiar brown Sheriff's Department uniform. Satisfied with what he showed her she picked up her desk phone and explained to the station manager the situation. In a short while, the station manager appeared and introduced herself to the deputy. She was young and had a fragile face and palmetto green eyes. She was well formed and wore a white blouse with a Budget Logo on her right shirt pocket; her dark brown skirt was unwrinkled. He produced his badge and ID once again and the young manager seemed satisfied. She made a few key strokes on her computer screen, pushed another button and a yellow sheet of paper rolled out of the printer that was sitting next to the computer. She pulled the copy from the printer and handed it to Tom. "I hope this is what you want," she said graciously and returned to her office.

Tom quickly glanced at the form he held in his hand. The car was leased by Joseph Diaz, P. O. Box 689, Ypsilanti, Michigan. He had been renting the car for the last six months and did not give a date when he would return it. The rental fee had been charged to his MasterCard. His address was given as room 202 at the Holiday Inn in Cedarton. After looking at the information he folded the print out and stuffed it in his shirt pocket. He left the Budget office satisfied he had discovered the name of the killer. The drive to Cedarton from the airport was forty minutes and when he arrived in Cedarton, he drove to the Holiday Inn, pulled into the parking lot, and located room 202. Diaz's car was not there but it didn't matter, he now knew where he lived.

The Sheriff was in his office when Tom arrived at the Law Enforcement Center. The young deputy knocked on his door and was invited in and offered a seat. Tom explained in more detail how he had sat next to the stranger in church and then followed him out of the church and watched him get into his car. Tom got up from his chair, pulled the folded printout from Budget and laid it on the Sheriff's desk. "Here's your killer."

"Good job. Now all you have to do is set up surveillance on our suspect and we'll see what his life is like in Cedarton. I'll let the deputies know to be on the lookout for this Tempo and you can contact Cedarton PD and have them watch the car and the hotel room. Something might come of this." The Sheriff called his secretary into his office, gave her the printout, and asked her to make a dozen copies and put them on my desk.

"I'll put in some extra hours for free, Sheriff. I am really anxious to catch this guy," Tom said, immediately realizing that it sounded stupid.

The Sheriff shook his head. "We'll leave things just as they are but I do appreciate your enthusiasm. We'll get him, trust me."

Tom understood and dropped the subject. "I'm going to run an NCIC check on this guy and see what we come up with." Within ten minutes, there was a reply on his search. It revealed nothing; Mr. Diaz had no felony arrests and there was no record of any criminal violations by him.

Tom returned to the Sheriff's office to say goodnight and tell the Sheriff about the NCIC search. "Oh, by the way, here's a receipt for ten dollars I had to pay at the airport to park the car."

According to the Cedarton police, they were watching the hotel and keeping an eye on the vehicle. Mr. Diaz was developing a pattern. He would leave the motel around midnight and drive to Bishop. The Bishop police watched him drive around their town until about two thirty. At precisely two-thirty, he would return to his hotel room. He would leave his hotel room again around noon and have lunch at the Perkins restaurant next door to the Holiday Inn. Every day he bought a paper and took it back to his room. He would not leave again until the following night. The pattern had been the same for the last three days. Tom felt confident that if Mr. Diaz was going to try anything, the deputies or police would be on him like flies to honey.

The first week in January ended and was one of the coldest on record. The pattern of Mr. Diaz had not altered and nothing out of the ordinary happened. After several more days of the same pattern, the vehicle suddenly disappeared from Cedarton and Bishop. The news was disconcerting and a thorough search of the county roads was undertaken; no sign of Diaz or his car was found. Another dead end, Tom thought to himself. He stopped at the Holiday Inn to check on room 202 and was told by the front desk clerk that the occupant of room 202 had checked out. Tom called the Budget office at the airport and talked to the manager who verified that he had returned the car. He checked with the airlines and discovered that Diaz had taken a Delta Air Lines fight to Michigan.

"He must have caught on what was happening and he left town," Tom was telling Josh as they were sitting in the squad room having a late morning cup of coffee.

"It's hard to figure, Tom. I mean, this guy has no record, no motive that we know about, and apparently did not know any of the victims. That's unusual. Why would someone come into our area, an area he doesn't know, kill six people and leave? You said you checked with the church members and the pastor and nobody said they knew him or had even seen him before."

"I know it sounds strange, but it is the only lead we've got," Tom answered.

"Well, there might be a chance he's our killer, but I'm not convinced. His movements are strange though, I'll give you that. He has been here for each of the murders; he leaves about midnight and returns at two-thirty which is about in the time frame that the murders took place. It is convincing evidence, but we need a lot more," Josh stated.

- 17 -

Easter would be late this year and not arrive until the third Sunday in April. The spring thaws had arrived, erasing all remaining remnants of snow. The trees were beginning to bud and the perennials were making their ascent from the ground. As Palm Sunday approached, the harsh winter weather had subsided and the long-range weather forecast was for clear skies and above normal temperatures. Spring in Minnesota, when it did finally arrive, was greeted with enthusiasm and excitement. The past winter, as with all winters, seemed unusually long. Winter had started early with the Halloween storm and continued up until the first week in April. Five months of cold weather was about all anybody could take before severe cabin fever began setting in.

The last three months had passed without incident for the Davis County Sheriff's Department. There had not been a felony committed. There had not been a murder or an attempted murder. Things were finally back to normal. In the back of the minds of the investigating team was the fact that since Joe Diaz left town things had certainly improved. Tom Jenks had contacted the Ypsilanti Sheriff's Department and inquired about Joe Diaz. He was informed they had no record on the man; he hadn't had as much as a speeding ticket. Tom asked if they would check into more details of his life and get back to him.

A couple of days later a report arrived from the Ypsilanti Police Department and Tom anxiously opened it. The report outlined a brief glimpse into the life of his prime suspect. Mr. Diaz, Joseph Carlos Diaz, was a clinical psychologist in Ypsilanti. He had a private practice and had an office in the downtown business district. His wife was a schoolteacher at the Jefferson grade school. The report went on to mention the vehicles registered to them, what church they attended, where they lived, how old the house was, his hobbies, the associations he belonged to, and where they both graduated from college. There was nothing in the report to show any kind of pattern that there was anything deviant in their lifestyle. This report, once again, stonewalled the investigation of Joe Diaz. The details of the report offered nothing that would show a motive for murder or explain the behavior of Joe Diaz. It was another frustrating dead end for the investigative team.

At two o'clock a.m. on Palm Sunday morning, the dispatchers at the law enforcement center received a 911 call.

"911 Emergency, go ahead."

"Yea, I just live down the road from the Helms place. You know the place where those murders took place. Yea, well, I watch the outside of the farm more than ever now and I kind of watch what's going on around the area, you know. Yea, well, I'm up getting a drink of water, I'm looking out the kitchen window, I see this car coming down the road with its headlights out, and it pulls into the Helms' driveway. It goes all the way up the driveway and pulls behind the storage shed. This guy gets out; he's alone. He walks to the house and goes in through the porch. That's when I called. I'm looking at the house now and he's still in there so can you send somebody out here quick?" The caller was nervous and excited as he related the information to the dispatcher.

"Could you hold, sir, while I contact a car?" The dispatcher put the caller on hold and informed all Sheriff's squads of a burglary in progress at the Helms farm. "The suspect vehicle is parked behind the storage shed and the suspect entered the house through the porch." All cars acknowledged and proceeded toward the farm, sirens silent and red lights off. The dispatcher got the necessary information from the caller and then focused her attention to monitoring the radio so she was aware at all times where the squad cars were and their status.

There were four squads on patrol that night and they all responded to the call. They approached the farmhouse and turned their headlights off. Bones was the first deputy on the scene and he waited at the entrance to the driveway for the other three deputies to arrive. The first two squad cars pulled in slowly and parked one on each side of the storage shed blocking the suspect vehicle. Bones was the third car in and he parked directly in front of the house while the fourth car blocked the driveway exit. The first two deputies got out of their cars and stood guard by the two exit doors of the house. When that was secure, Bones shined his spotlights on the house. He announced over the loudspeaker that they were the Sheriff's Department and he was to come out and surrender.

"We know you are in there. We have the place surrounded. You might as well give yourself up and come out peacefully," Bones commanded.

Bones waited patiently and three times called to the burglar to come out. After the third try, he warned the suspect that he had five minutes to come out of the house or that they would have to come in and get him. The five minutes went by without a sign the burglar was coming out.

Bones entered the house first, while another deputy followed a few feet behind. Bones was not sure if the electricity worked because the house hadn't been lived in since the murders. It didn't matter, he decided he didn't want any lights on and the two deputies used only their flashlights. Bones and the other deputy slowly and carefully inspected each room. After the first floor was completely done they went upstairs and cautiously walked through each room. They checked all of the bedrooms; they looked under the beds, into the closets and into the hall closet, and finally checked the upstairs bathroom. So far, they had come up with nothing. Bones knew the burglar had to be in the house or one of the outbuildings. If he was in an outbuilding, it would be hard for him to escape. The yard was lit up by flood lights and the burglar's car was blocked in. Bones was sure he was in the house; they just hadn't found him yet.

"What's left?" the deputy whispered to Bones.

"I don't know; just let me think a second. There has got to be someplace. Did you notice a door in the kitchen? I did, I think it leads to the fruit cellar. I'd forgotten about that; come on," Bones commanded to the other deputy.

Bones was the first one down the narrow stairway to the fruit cellar. Each step creaked and if someone was in the fruit cellar they had to be aware someone was coming down the steps. Shining his flashlight around he noticed some shelving with canned fruits or vegetables in the jars, he wasn't sure but it appeared they were covered in dust. To the right of the shelving were a washer and dryer. Bones directed his flashlight behind the washer first and then raised the beam of the flashlight toward the dryer. The light focused on the face of a man crouching behind it. Both Bones and the deputy pointed their flashlights into his face. They had their guns drawn and aimed at the suspect.

"Put your hands on top of your head and stand up slowly, very slowly and keep your hands above your head," Bones commanded.

The burglar did as he was ordered, slowing rising so as not to alarm the deputies that he was going to make any sudden moves.

"See if there is a light switch somewhere near the stairs and try turning it on," Bones ordered and hoped that the electricity was still on. "I want to get a good look at this guy." The deputy found the switch at the top of the stairs and flicked it. Two small light bulbs lit up and Bones was in a better position to look at the suspect. Bones directed the suspect to walk slowly over to the wall, place his hands on the wall as far apart as he could and step back from the wall and spread his feet.

"Put your feet back more and spread your legs more," Bone directed, wanting the burglar to be in a position so that if he tried to stand up and run he would be unbalanced to do so. Bones held his gun on the burglar and told the deputy to cuff him. After he was safely cuffed, Bones asked him his name.

"Joe Diaz, Sir."

"Joe Diaz, you are under arrest. You have the right to remain silent. Anything you say can and will be used against you in a court of law. You have the right to an attorney and if you cannot afford one, one will be provided for you. Do you understand these rights?"

"I do sir."

He put the Miranda card back in his shirt pocket and the two deputies escorted Diaz to Bones' squad car.

Bones grabbed the mike and informed dispatch that they had the suspect in custody and would be returning to the station. "Please call the Sheriff and advise him of the situation. Tell him the individual we have in custody is the one we have been watching," Bones stated calmly.

Bones pulled into the sally port; the prisoner safely handcuffed in the rear seat. The single car garage was connected to the booking room and a jailer would be waiting for him and the suspect. Cameras were on the prisoner from the time he exited the squad car until he entered the booking room where a new set of cameras took over. The prisoner was turned over to the jailer who booked him in and escorted him to a holding cell. After the prisoner was safely inside the jail, Bones backed his car out of the sally port and pulled it next to the Sheriff's unmarked squad car.

Sheriff Bean met Bones at the door as he was coming in. The Sheriff was in his street clothes and looked a little disheveled. *He must have come down to the station right away and didn't bother to freshen up*, Bones thought to himself when he first saw the Sheriff.

"What'ya got Bones?" the Sheriff asked; he appeared tired.

"We stopped a burglary in progress at the Helms farm and guess who we found inside? One Joseph Diaz. He is being booked right now."

"I want you to do your reports right away so we can go over them in the morning," the Sheriff ordered. "We are not going to talk to Diaz tonight. We'll let him get a good night sleep and we'll interview him sometime tomorrow. Let's keep him guessing as to what's going on."

The Sheriff would call Josh, Tom, and Frank in the morning and fill them in on all the details.

- 18 -

Three weeks prior, Sylvia Pennington celebrated her thirty-third birthday with a close friend and confidante, Sam Taylor. She was surprised when he called her a day before her birthday and offered to buy her supper to celebrate the 'big event'. Sylvia wasn't aware that Sam even knew when her birthday was; they worked together but she didn't think it ever came up in their many conversations together. It didn't matter, she had nothing planned and gladly accepted his offer. After getting off the phone Sam Taylor excitedly called Gideon's and made reservations for two for the following evening.

Gideon's was a favorite restaurant of Sylvia's and she looked forward to her date with Sam. They had been friends for many years and she never felt an urge to be more than friends until her divorce. She was thirty-two years old, single for the first time in eleven years and beginning a new life.

The short drive to Cedarton was uneventful; Sylvia made small talk with Sam and he did the same. The undersized parking lot at Gideon's was half-full and as Sam pulled into the parking lot he noticed an open space near the front door. He eased in, got out of the car, promptly walked to the other side, and opened the door for his date. Once inside and seated Sam retrieved a birthday card from his inside jacket pocket and handed to Sylvia. She smiled at Sam as she opened the card and looked inside. An iTunes gift card dropped out and landed on the table. She picked it up, looked at it, then got up from her chair, walked over to Sam, and kissed him on the cheek. This was to be one of the best birthdays she had since she married John. She would see a lot more of Sam Taylor; she was certain of that.

She stood in front of the bathroom mirror looking at herself as she ran a brush through her chestnut colored hair. Her aquiline features with the small pointed nose and sturdy cheekbones complemented her long black hair, her small forehead, and dark hazel eyes. She was proud of her hair and had worked hard to get it to look like it did right now. She fussed over it, running the brush through it many times. The thick bristles of the hairbrush felt good against her head and with each stroke of the brush, she realized more and more how happy she finally was. Her skin tone, a stunning bronze added to her beauty. She looked more Polynesian than her white Scandinavian ancestry should have allowed.

Her tumultuous marriage to John Pennington endured for eleven years. It had been a troubled marriage for the last nine and it was on New Years Eve, two years into their marriage that the accident happened. They had left a house party in the early morning hours and both had been drinking heavily. They were encouraged by their friends not to drive but John was adamant that he was okay. Her husband was driving faster than he should have, and Sylvia begged him to slow down but her pleas fell on deaf ears.

They had come to the last curve before their home when he lost control of the vehicle and slammed into a guardrail on the left side of the road. The car smashed through the guardrail and overturned. It was at the hospital that Sylvia learned her husband had suffered a broken neck, while she had luckily escaped with only minor cuts and scratches.

Her husband was a quadriplegic. Sylvia was by his side every day during his long and difficult recuperation. She offered him her love, her support and her dedication in hopes that it would ease and maybe even hasten his recovery. When he finally came home from the rehab center, his attitude had improved slightly from what it had been in the hospital. But he easily became frustrated, angry, and bitter and wouldn't talk for days. Sylvia had been told by the doctor this was normal under the circumstances and that after a time his mental condition would improve as he accepted his fate and directed his energies into overcoming his handicap as best he could. As the months and years passed by, his embittered attitude worsened; it seemed to Sylvia that he would never accept his handicap. His anger was ceaseless and he directed his hostilities toward those closest to him. Sylvia received the brunt of it and it was starting to take a toll on her both physically and mentally. His words were cutting and many times he would drive her to tears. He was not able to physically harm her but he knew that he could psychologically destroy her. She had grown to hate her husband because of the suffering and pain he was causing her. She finally moved into a separate bedroom and only did the minimum duties required to nurse him. She wouldn't make his bed for three or four days and would cook him food he didn't like. She would irritate him in any way she could. Finally, she decided that it wasn't worth it anymore and she had to get along with their life. She filed for divorce, left the house, and moved into an apartment. She arranged for his care until the court ruled on the division of property. The Judge ruled that Sylvia would get the house but she allowed her ex-husband to stay until there was an opening at the County nursing home.

Finishing up in the bathroom, she walked into the kitchen, poured herself a cup of coffee, and sat down at the counter to read the Bishop Gazette. It was her day to do as she wished; it was her day off and she was going to enjoy it. She was in the mood for reading a good book and going for a nice long walk. Finishing her coffee and newspaper, she placed the empty cup in the sink and went to the hall closet, grabbed a warm sweater and put it on. She walked outside, inhaled the fresh spring air, and began her journey. She was happy and free and her mind was clear, able to focus on more positive things now that she had erased John from her memory. She noticed that every street in Bishop had a sidewalk; she had walked the streets many times but never noticed them before. She was aware for the first time how big the oak tree in Jake Peters' back yard really was. *It must be at least a hundred years old* she thought to herself. All throughout the town and on every street she was seeing things as she had never seen them before. For some reason she felt enlightened and euphoric this morning. She stopped at the park, which she had never done before, and spent the good part of an hour just watching people and their peculiar mannerisms. Her next stop was the library and she just somehow knew that a good book would be waiting there. Ten minutes later, she walked out of the library with a John Sandford mystery under her arm. The rest of the day would be spent reading. The ambiance of her small living room would have been enhanced and the mood perfected for reading if there was a fireplace with a large crackling fire and a dog sleeping at her feet. It was not to be and she was satisfied sitting on her couch with a warm blanket covering her, her feet folded underneath her body. Time passed quickly, she had read over a hundred pages and decided to check to see what time it was. It was five o'clock. *Where had the time gone* she thought to herself. Her date with Sam was at seven; she better begin getting ready. She put the book down on the coffee table in front of the couch, stretched her arms, yawned and then got up and went to the bathroom to take a shower. She was feeling exuberant about her date with Sam and hoped they would have an enjoyable evening. She turned off the water and stepped out of the shower, gently wiping the water from her body. She slowly applied body lotion over herself, put on a bathrobe, walked to the stereo, and put on her favorite Beatles album. Satisfied with the volume of the music, she went to the bedroom, turned off the lights, and lay on the bed, her mind blank.

She was lying on the bed, listening to 'Imagine' when suddenly a cloth-like material was stuffed into her mouth and a strip of tape quickly and carelessly placed over her mouth. A cold, sharp object touched her throat; she guessed it was a knife. The intruder warned her to be quiet or he would kill her. Her eyes widened with horror, trying to grasp what was happening. She kept still and quiet, obeying the words of her captor. She was sure she was going to be raped but didn't want to be harmed in any other way. A profile of the man's face became visible to her as she tried to make out who he was. She felt the sharp object leave her throat and she felt relieved; he wasn't going to harm her. The man leaned down and whispered in her ear.

"I've been talking to John quite a bit lately; he told me all about you and your little tricks," the intruder started. "He told me that you have been quite mean to him. He says you did everything in your power to make his life more miserable than what it already was. He told me you stopped cleaning the house and that you wouldn't make his bed. He says you did this to annoy him. He had to lie in his own filth for days on end until you decided to change the sheets and give him a clean bed to lie in. He also told me about the meals, he said that you would only cook food for him that disgusted him. You knew what food he hated and that is what you served him. And then Sylvia, after messing with him like that, you divorced him and put him in a nursing home. What kind of person are you, Sylvia?"

She lay there, as still as she was able to be but trembling and unable to answer because of the tape over her mouth. She stared at the intruder, trying to figure out who he was. He had to know both her and John. His voice seemed familiar.

"What are we going to do about this little problem Sylvia? He says that you have even been messing around with another guy lately. He's right you know. You see, I watched your house last night and you had some man over. What were you doing, playing tiddely winks? I think not, Sylvia. After watching your place last night I know that John was telling me the truth. How many guys

172

have there been since the divorce, or maybe you were messing around while you were married. You were, weren't you?"

Sylvia shook her head from side to side indicating to the intruder that he was wrong. She felt the sharp object next to her throat again only this time it punctured the skin and she could feel the warm blood as it found its way down her neck. She was more scared now than she had ever been in her life. Anger replaced fear and she reached out with both of her legs and kicked the intruder. The kick caught him in the groin and he doubled up with pain. She kicked him again sending him backwards and onto the floor. She got up from the bed and began running to the door when he grabbed her by the hair and dragged her to the floor. She felt the pain of his fists pounding on her face until she felt no more and everything went blank. When she woke up, she was on the bed. Her arms were tied to the bed board, her legs spread apart and tied to the metal legs at the bottom of the bed.

"Don't pull any more tricks like that or I'll kill you," he said, his voice emitting a coldness that it hadn't before. "Now don't lie to me Sylvia, how much whoring around did you do on John while you were married?"

She again shook her head from side to side hoping she could convince him that he was wrong. She could feel perspiration run down her cheeks and hoped it was only perspiration and not blood.

"How about since your divorce?" he asked, his face coming near her as he waited for the answer.

She did nothing, only stared at the stranger trying to figure out what this was all about. She didn't think John would hire somebody to kill her or beat her up. He had a temper and might have gone off the deep end; she hated him at this moment more than she ever had.

"You didn't answer my question, Sylvia. Who you been seeing?" the intruder asked, this time his voice was one of hate, anger and impatience.

The coldness in his voice was still there and Sylvia now realized this man was going to kill her. She lay motionless looking at the stranger. He stood over her, quiet, staring at her with an evil smile on his face. It was then that she recognized him and tried to scream. She saw the knife come down toward her. She gasped for air briefly and then she was no more. Her life in an instant had been taken away.

The bloodied knife was now being used to cut the beautiful chestnut hair that his victim had been so proud of. When most of the hair had been sheared off, he removed a gold bracelet she had been wearing on her right ankle. The killer lifted the bracelet, stuffed what hair he could through it, and placed it on the nightstand by the bed. He removed a calling card from his shirt pocket and placed it on the nightstand next to the bracelet and hair. It read 'DEATH. ON. OTHERS. BY. LIVING. EVIL.' It would be his last murder. Satisfied that everything was in its place he removed a small towel from his front pants pocket, wiped the knife clean, and returned it to its sheath. He carefully inspected the bedroom, vigilantly looking for any signs of evidence he might have left when the phone next to the bed rang. Surprised, he hurriedly scanned the room one final time. Satisfied everything was as it should be, he turned on the lamp that was sitting on the nightstand and left. He walked out the rear door, removed his surgical gloves, put them in his pocket and walked toward his car careful not to been seen by anyone.

Sam Taylor was hurt and disappointed that Sylvia had stood him up. She was to meet him at the Torchlight Restaurant. He waited for over a half an hour and when she didn't come he got worried. He had tried calling her several times with no luck, only getting the answering machine. He left a message for her to call him as soon as she got home. He had fallen in love with Sylvia several years ago. Now that she had gotten a divorce, he had the opportunity he had always dreamed of. He waited for her call but it never came.

He didn't sleep well that night. He was confused, acting like an adolescent who had discovered love for the first time. He was heartbroken she had stood him up when she had promised him they would be together for the evening. She could have at least returned his call, he thought as his mind tried to think up a dozen excuses why she hadn't. He decided to go over to her house tomorrow morning and demand an explanation.

The Sheriff, along with Josh, Tom, and Frank were making final preparations for their interview with Joe Diaz when the call came in. It was received by the dispatch office at 1031 hours and was made by Sam Taylor who was calling from the home of Sylvia Pennington.

- 19 -

The Sheriff and the dooble team were excited, ebullient, and maybe a little bit giddy, but most of all they felt an overwhelming sense of relief. They finally had a suspect, a good suspect. All they needed to do was put the pieces of the puzzle together and they then could get an arrest warrant. Joe Diaz had to be their man. Their joy was short lived when the phone call came into the Law Enforcement Sunday morning. There had been another murder and if everything held true, the murder was committed sometime between two and three in the morning. Joe Diaz was in jail.

The Sheriff contacted his team soon after the initial investigation of Sylvia Pennington's death and set up a meeting for Monday morning. *Where would they go from here*, the Sheriff asked himself. Sometime during half-time of the Minnesota Vikings game, the Sheriff received a call from the pathologist. He placed the time of death for Sylvia Pennington at seven-thirty pm Saturday night. The murder had taken place a full six hours before Diaz was arrested at the Helms farm. They were back on course in the investigation. Diaz could have easily killed the Pennington woman before he was apprehended and the Sheriff was anxious to relay the information to his team.

Monday morning Tom Jenks, Frank Blume, and Josh walked into the Sheriff's office. Each routinely poured a cup of coffee, exchanged their "good mornings", and took their seats. When Sheriff Bean announced the time of death of Sylvia Pennington, the mood in the room changed. Realizing what this meant, their excitement was renewed. They talked about what needed to be done next and who needed to do what. They were now more than certain they had the right man behind bars. The Sheriff and Josh were going to interview Joe Diaz after their meeting and hoped the interview would go well. "Diaz would probably 'lawyer up'," Josh offered. "But maybe not right away."

"Let's also hope our next meeting will be to celebrate Diaz' arrest for murder," the Sherriff said.

"I'm pretty sure the murders will end, whether it was Joe Diaz or somebody else. Pennington was the last one, according to his calling card. So, either Diaz is our man and he's locked up or our serial killer is somebody else and he has fulfilled his mission," Josh related to the team.   "It is not my opinion alone; our psychiatrist at the Bureau agrees. You know, Sheriff, we have tried to get a psychological makeup on this guy but haven't had much luck. There is no pattern in these murders that are similar with any other serial killings that have been studied. If he'd performed some kind of sex act with the victims, it would indicate a lot of things and allow a profile to work.   Not one of the victims was sexually assaulted or molested in any way. Let's just hope Diaz is our man and we can add a new chapter to the study of serial killers."

The Sheriff turned to Frank and Tom. "You guys weren't at the investigation, but the modus operandi was the same as every other murder. The killer must have had more time on this one. The hair had been cut off the victim very neatly, unlike the haphazard way it was done with some of the victims. Maybe he was more confident this time. Well, anyway, he took the last victim's hair and pulled it through a bracelet and set it neatly on the table beside her bed. He then placed his now infamous calling card under the bracelet. The Sheriff passed the card around the room for the team to look at; it was enclosed in a clear plastic evidence bag and could be easily read. 'DEATH. ON. OTHERS. BY. LIVING. EVIL.' As you guys can see, the calling card is now complete."

Frank turned to Josh, "So, the time of death was around seven-thirty."

"That's right, several hours before your deputies arrested Diaz."

"I wonder why he changed his routine?" Tom innocently asked.

"Not only did he change his routine but he killed inside the city limits of Bishop for the first time. All of the other murders were in secluded areas where his chances of being seen were minimal. We need to find out what was so different about Sylvia Pennington that the killer would alter his routine," Josh replied.

"How about her church, Josh. Did she belong to the Abundant Life Church?" the Sheriff asked.

"Nope. Another inconsistency. She didn't belong to any church."

"How about your search warrants, Frank?" the Sheriff asked.

"The County Attorney has the warrants for the car and motel room done and should be signed by the Judge sometime this afternoon. The car is impounded and no one has gone near it. He's not staying at the Holiday Inn in Cedarton anymore; he has moved to the Holiday Inn Airport. I contacted the manager of the Holiday Inn Airport and he told me that he would personally seal the room off until we arrived and did what we had to do."

"Good and you will take care of that, Frank?" the Sheriff questioned.

"Don't worry about it. I'll take care of it. Tom's going with me."

"Do you have anything to add, Josh?" the Sheriff asked.

"Just to fill you in briefly. We found no evidence at the Pennington scene. We talked to the neighbors and one of them remembered the light going on in the bedroom around seven-thirty, but that's it. None of the other neighbors saw anything. It was dark and they were all watching television or occupied with other things. She was murdered with possibly the same knife but the pathologist tells me there are some inconsistencies so he can't verify if it was the same knife or not. The pathology reports show the exact size of the wound and cut and it appears the same knife may have been used. The pathologist says she died instantly. Not much else to tell you right now."

The Sheriff picked up the phone, called the jail, and asked the jailor to bring the inmate Diaz to his office. He hung up the phone and told Frank and Tom they could leave. "When the warrants are signed, serve them right away. We have no time to waste."

"Good luck with Diaz," they said as they walked out of the Sheriff's office.

Joe Diaz appeared at the door of Sheriff Bean's office. He was wearing handcuffs and leg irons. The jailor directed him where to sit.

"Thanks, you can go now. Please close the door," the Sheriff said matter-of-factly, more for the prisoners benefit than to sound stern to the jailor.

The Sheriff would not have recognized Joe Diaz from what he remembered from the videos. The prisoner hadn't shaved since his arrest; the black stubble on his face, the tousled hair, and the wrinkled jail uniform were a far cry from the clean-shaven and neat appearing man he had seen at the church. His eyes were bloodshot and he needed a shower.

Josh began the interrogation, "Mr. Diaz, I am going to read you your Miranda warning. I know it was read to you on the night of your arrest, but I want to make sure you understand it." Josh read him the warning and when the prisoner heard it, he politely stated that he understood it fully.

"Now, Mr. Diaz, before we start, I must tell you that our interview is going to be videotaped," Josh said as he pointed to two cameras, one in each corner of the office behind the Sheriff's desk. Joe Diaz looked at each of the cameras and said nothing.

"What is your full name?"

"Joseph Carlos Diaz"

"Where do you live?"

"I am staying at the Holiday Inn in Minneapolis for now, but my home address is 3722 Meadowlark Lane, Ypsilanti, Michigan."

"What do you do for a living?"

"I'm a clinical psychologist in Ypsilanti."

"Who do you work for?"

"I'm self employed and have an office in downtown Ypsilanti."

"Do you have a family?"

"Yes. I have a wife, Cathy, and two living daughters and one deceased daughter."

"Have you contacted your wife?"

"No, I am not ready yet."

"Okay, Mr. Diaz. Do you know why you are here?"

"Yes. I was arrested inside of a house. I guess you call it burglary."

"That's right. Why were you there?"

"I was looking for something."

"What?"

"I can't say at this time."

"What did you plan to steal?"

"Nothing, believe me. I didn't break into the house to steal anything. Surely you must have noticed that nothing was out of place in the house when you did your investigation."

"Why didn't you come out when the deputies asked you to?"

"I was scared and I was nervous. I had never been in that kind of situation before. I just froze. I wasn't thinking straight. When I heard the cars coming into the driveway I went into the basement and hid."

"Joe, you have been hanging around Bishop off and on for quite some time now. In fact, a large part of last year you lived in our county doing heaven knows what. You suddenly checked out of your motel room in Cedarton, left the area and now you are back again. Do you want to explain all this, because I am really interested."

"I was checking out the area. I am thinking of moving my practice to Cedarton. This seems like such a nice place."

"Yea, sure," the Sheriff answered sarcastically and changed the subject. "Joe, you have been seen at the Abundant Life Church for each of the services of the murder victims. Why?"

"I read about those murders and just wanted to show up and offer my condolences."

"I don't believe you Joe."

"I don't understand what you are getting at. First of all, my being here for the past six months and my attending that church has nothing to do with the burglary. So what are you getting at?"

"Let's put it this way. There are a lot of coincidences in these murders and your behavior. Every murder we've had has happened while you were here. When you left, the murders stopped. When you returned, we had another murder."

"You talking about that Pennington lady that got murdered? That story was all over the radio this morning."

"Yea, Joe, we are."

"How could you even try and connect me with that murder? I was in jail."

"Sorry, Joe, but you weren't. The murder happened at seven thirty last night and you weren't arrested for several hours later."

"She was killed at seven thirty? That can't be," Joe stated. He seemed startled at the time the murder happened. It was the only show of emotion he had up until now.

"You know something, don't you?"

"I know nothing about those murders. If you are going to continue questioning me about them, I will invoke my Miranda privileges and discontinue this conversation," Joe said. Both the Sheriff and Josh noticed he was nervous and appeared more agitated at the direction the questioning was taking.

"I hope you can see where we are coming from, Joe. First of all, every murder happened while you were in the area. You show up for every funeral service. You travel around the area every night from midnight until about two thirty and then return to your motel room. The murders all took place before two thirty so that gives you opportunity. You leave the area and bingo, no more murders. You come back and guess what, another murder. On top of all that, you are caught in the house where the first murders took place. The circumstances are piling up and we are very close to getting a murder indictment for you. Why not cooperate now, it will help you in the long run Mr. Diaz."

"I know it looks fishy, but believe me, I didn't kill anyone."

"Do you know who did?"

"No."

"Why did you pick that particular house to burglarize?"

"I told you I was looking for something."

"But you won't tell us what?"

"No. Look, you got me dead to rights. You found me in the house and you are charging me with burglary. What else do you want? I'm invoking my rights under Miranda and don't want to talk anymore."

The Sheriff entered the conversation, "Tomorrow at eleven thirty, you will have your first appearance in front of the Judge. He will read the charges to you and also inform you of what the penalties are for your crime. You will then enter a plea of guilty or not guilty. Bail will be set. We are going to ask for a high bail, even though it is only a burglary charge. You understand that you are a prime suspect in our murder investigation and you do live out of state. The Judge will take that into consideration when he sets bail. If you plead not guilty, you will be asked if you want an attorney. If you can't afford an attorney, the court will appoint one for you..."

Joe interrupted "I can afford an attorney."

"..If you can't post bail," the Sheriff continued, "you will be brought back to the jail. I would suggest that you get an attorney. At least he can persuade the Judge to lower your bail, if nothing else."

"I guess I am going to need an attorney. I can easily afford one. Is there a good defense lawyer in the area?"

"I really can't tell you who to pick, but if it was me and I was in your kind of trouble I'd contact Ivan Stoner. He's good. We call him Ivan the Terrible, because he's a tyrant in court when it comes to defending his clients," the Sheriff said, as he pulled out one of Ivan Stoner's business cards from the front drawer of his desk and handed it to Joe Diaz.

Joe Diaz accepted the card and looked at it before putting in the front pocket of his orange jump suit. "Thanks. I'll give him a call."

The Sheriff stood up, contacted the jailor through the intercom, and asked him to come to his office and return Mr. Diaz to his cell. After Joe Diaz was escorted back to the jail, the Sheriff asked Josh what he thought of the whole situation.

"Either he did the murders, or he knows who did them."

"That's what I think too."

"We'll know more when Frank gets back from his search warrants, but I think we may have enough circumstantial evidence to charge him now. He knows something. If he didn't do it, he just may talk to us and try and save his ass."

That evening Ivan Stoner showed up at the law enforcement center and asked to speak to his client, Joe Diaz.

- 20 -

The Sheriff leaned back in his soft red leather chair and gazed at the coffee cup sitting on his desk. A cloud of steam emanated from its contents providing an aroma the Sheriff desperately needed this morning. He enjoyed the smell but delayed his first sip until it cooled down a bit. He rubbed his forehead trying to ease the throbbing in his head. He felt like he had been run over by a Peterbilt.   But he hadn't; he had been drinking with Josh Trimble the night before, drinking way too much and way too late. He was now paying for his sins and would do so for most of the day. He was about to take his first sip of the hot coffee when his intercom buzzed. "Sheriff, there is a Captain Bartholomew here to see you."

"I don't know any Captain Bartholomew."

"He says he knows you from the restaurant."

He was struggling to remember where he had heard the name Captain Bartholomew before but his mind wasn't performing as well as it should. It finally came to him as he remembered the incident at the restaurant and the strange conversation with the man in the army uniform.

"Send him in."

He hand was mildly shaking as he lifted the coffee cup to his lips when the Captain appeared in the doorway. He stood motionless for a second before walking to the center of the small office and saluted the Sheriff. *I don't need this shit so early in the morning.*

Bartholomew dropped his salute, studying the Sheriff trying to get a feel for his mood. "Good morning, Sheriff Bean."

"Good morning Bartholomew. Have a seat," the Sheriff said, gesturing to one of the chairs in his office. Bartholomew continued standing, facing the Sheriff, not saying a word.

"Something wrong?"

"Yes. First of all, you will recognize my position. I am Captain Bartholomew and I expect you to address me as such. You will have the same respect for my title and uniform as I have for yours. I don't call you Milo, do I? I call you Sheriff Bean, so please oblige me with the same courtesies."

"Yea, Yea," the Sheriff muttered, talking to himself more than to the man standing in front of him. "Please have a seat Captain Bartholomew and tell me what is on your mind. I have a lot of work this morning so please make it short."

Bartholomew accepted this request and sat down; his posture erect. He sat motionless and quiet waiting for the Sheriff to start the conversation. When he didn't, Captain Bartholomew spoke up. "I know who your murderer is."

Curious, the Sheriff sat up in his chair and moved it closer to his desk. He placed both hands on his desk and looked at the Captain. "You have my full attention, please continue."

Bartholomew pulled a knife out of the sheath he was wearing on his army belt and placed it on the Sheriff's desk. "Here's the murder weapon. It's a...."

"I know what it is, I was issued one when I was in Nam. There must have been millions of these knives made. Where did you get this one?"

"The murderer gave it to my brother," Bartholomew replied calmly, his flushed face slowly turning to crimson as he was getting angrier with the Sheriff for his seemingly lackadaisical attitude. "There are no prints on the knife; it has been wiped clean."

The Sheriff took out an 11 x 14 lined legal pad and placed it in front of him, prepared to write. "I want to get all this down so please go slow."

Bartholomew nodded his approval and began. "If you check that knife out, you will find that its size will be consistent with the knife marks left on the victims. My brother gave me that knife to give to you. He said you would know what to do with it. My brother told me that at each one of the funerals there was this guy sitting in the front pew. He was at all the funerals, just sitting there staring at my brother. My brother didn't know who he was but thought this was kind of strange. After the Mattie Blake funeral, he approached this man and asked him to please come to his office after the service. Well, the guy shows up at my brother's office and they start talking about why he is there. He is reluctant and is crying. He breaks down and tells my brother that he killed all those people and that he came to the funeral out of guilt feelings. He wanted to make things right by offering his condolences. My brother is aghast by this admission of guilt and tries to console this guy who he soon finds out is Joe Diaz. Mr. Diaz apparently goes into great detail about the murders and talked about his hatred for women. He spends about two hours with my brother and my brother finally convinces him that God will forgive his sins but he has to give him the murder weapon as a sign that he will purge himself of any more murders. This Diaz guy makes a promise that he won't do this again, but he wants more convincing that his sins would be forgiven. My brother assures him that their conversation is sacred and privileged and promises not to tell anyone. "I have taken a vow of secrecy in these matters, your confession is between only you and me and God, and I won't break my vows." My brother tells him, though, that if he does it again, he will have to rethink his vows and maybe notify the authorities. When the Pennington woman was killed, my brother decided that he would have to report this to me. That's why I'm here."

The Sheriff didn't need this so early in the morning. The actions of Bartholomew were confusing and he was uncertain about the credibility of what he was being told.

"You and your brother are pretty close, aren't you? I admire that." It was the best the Sheriff could offer.

"He's my brother and also my best friend."

"You say Diaz gave your brother the knife after the Blake murder, but yet another murder happened in the same way. The victim was murdered with a knife. How do you explain that?"

Captain Bartholomew, annoyed at the Sheriff's line of questioning shifted in his chair and looked angrily at the Sheriff. "Logic would tell us that he used a different knife, Sheriff. Do you think maybe we should talk to Trimble about this and let him handle it instead of you?"

The Sheriff ignored the last question and continued. "Did Diaz say why he was in Bishop, so far away from his home in Ypsilanti?"

Bartholomew glared at the Sheriff, his dark brown eyes, cold, and calculating. He appeared miffed. "Diaz is from Ypsilanti, Michigan? I didn't know that and I can't answer that question."

"If your brother talked to him for a couple of hours, he must have told him more about the murders than you are telling me now. You say his motive was the fact that he hated women. Not many people go around killing women just because they hate them. If they do kill them, there would be some kind of sexual assault to go along with it," the Sheriff stopped, realizing that maybe he was telling Bartholomew more than he should.

"I can't answer much more, Sheriff. My brother has left the rest of his conversation with Diaz in secrecy and wouldn't tell me any more."

"Why didn't your brother come in himself?"

"He's a very busy man and he just didn't have time. He trusted me to handle this."

"Are you going to be available to talk in case we have more questions? Where can I reach you?"

"I'm going to be hard to get a hold of. I'll call occasionally."

"You know, Captain, this is the evidence we need to get a murder warrant for Diaz. We're going to have to talk with your brother, though. Can you arrange that?"

"No, you're going to have to talk to me only," Captain Bartholomew replied, anxious to leave before any more questions were asked.

"Would you take a polygraph, Captain?" the Sheriff asked, wondering what the Captains response would be. "This new evidence is so important we need to verify it to get the warrant."

"A polygraph test is not admissible in court, Sheriff, and you know it so don't play games with me."

"I'm not talking about court. But if the test confirms what you are saying is true we might be able to get around the hearsay rule and have enough probable cause for the issuance of the warrant. See what I am getting at?"

Bartholomew's frigid eyes glared at the Sheriff. "I am not taking any damn lie detector test. From now on I want to talk to Trimble alone. You're getting too old and senile for this job. This case is way beyond your pay grade so let somebody handle it that is capable. I gave you the murder weapon, for Pete's sake. You should be thrilled to death." Bartholomew was almost shouting now as he got up from his chair to leave. "If you don't charge Diaz with those murders, I will make it awful damn miserable for you around this town. I will let everybody know you've got the murder weapon and are bungling this case in a big way. I can do it and you know it. People are already fed up with you." He walked out and slammed the office door behind him.

The Sheriff carefully picked up the knife, walked down the hallway to Josh's office, and went in without knocking. Josh was sitting at his desk reading the morning paper. He had it turned to the business section.

"How're your stocks doing, Rockefeller?"

"Doing well. I'm making some money finally."

The Sheriff laid the knife on his desk and asked if he recognized it.

"Sure do. It is a standard issue army knife. There were millions of them made. We had a similar knife in the Marines, but, of course, it was a better quality," Josh joked.

The Sheriff went into detail about his conversation with Bartholomew. "What kind of a guy do you think this is? I mean, he was just as cocksure of himself now as he was in the restaurant. He thinks I am a bungling idiot and wants you to take over the whole case and leave me out of it. I don't know how two people out of the same family can be so different. He talks a lot about his brother though, so they must get along pretty good, but I don't for the life of me see how they can."

"I don't know, Sheriff. He strikes me as one of those short little bastards that carry a grudge on their shoulders because they are so small, you know the Napoleon complex at its finest. I have met a lot of them, it's like they've got something to prove, you know, as if they are as good as anybody else or even better. I think his height has a lot to do with his attitude."

"He tells me this is the murder weapon," the Sheriff said, pointing to the knife on the desk. "Supposedly, it has been wiped clean. Bartholomew didn't tell me who wiped it - Diaz, the pastor, or him."

"I'll get this to our lab to see if it matches the wounds on the victims. One thing interesting about the knife wounds, though. All the victims, except Pennington, were killed with a similar weapon. Her wounds were made with a different knife, a smaller one, probably a hunting knife."

"That's consistent with Bartholomew telling me that Diaz gave this knife to the pastor after the Blake murder," the Sheriff pointed out, wondering if maybe Bartholomew knew a lot more about Diaz than he was letting on.

Josh was lighting a cigarette when his phone rang. It was Frank Blume, calling from the Holiday Inn in Minneapolis. Josh searched for and finally found a piece of paper to write on. He jotted down several things and then hung up and looked at the Sheriff. "Here's what they found on the warrants for Diaz. In the hotel room, they found a calligraphy set but nothing else. They confiscated it for evidence. In the trunk of his vehicle, they found a hunting knife with traces of blood. Frank is taking it to our lab right now as long as he's in Minneapolis anyway. That way too, he won't break the chain of evidence. Nothing else was found. But if the blood matches Sylvia Pennington's, we've got enough probable cause for a warrant."

What a morning this has been, Milo thought to himself. *Screw Bartholomew, they were going to get the warrant without his help*. He was leaving Josh's office with an excitement he hadn't felt since the murders started. He was at the door, ready to leave when Josh stood up and laughingly asked, "Hey, Sheriff, want to go down for a couple of drinks tonight?"

Milo looked at him; the smile had left his face and was replaced with one of dismay. He walked back to his office without answering.

- 21 -

Whenever Ivan Stoner rose from the defense table to address the jury or to question a witness the courtroom fell silent. Once in a while, you could hear a soft whisper from the audience but that would be a rare occurrence. His deep voice with its pleasant and articulate timbre captivated an audience. His six foot four inch frame was solidly built and he had hands that were large enough to cover half a football. He wore expensive clothing and expensive jewelry; he could easily afford it. His black hair had streaks of gray running through it which seemed to enhance his appearance. It hung down to his shoulders and clung to his suit like a magnet. Earlier, when his career was just beginning he wore his hair in a ponytail but it didn't take long to discover that his hairstyle distracted the jury; looking like a hippy in a conservative town didn't sit well with the panel of jurors watching and listening and judging the young defense attorney. The ponytail never won a case and it didn't take him long to figure out why.

He was one of the most liberal leaning persons in Davis County with the exception of Bill Johnson, the coffee clutch participant at the Bishop Cafe. He was chairman of the county Democratic Party and had been for the past two years; he was also secretary for the State Democratic-Farmer-Laborer party, a definite minority party in Davis County. Ivan Stoner was determined to change that. He was as passionate about his politics as he was about the legal profession and generously supported every organization that espoused his philosophy. He had become very wealthy by winning several product liability suits throughout the state. He disliked corporations and savored each victory he won for his clients.

"Your Honor, we are ready to proceed with this hearing," Stoner began.

"Have you discussed with your client to his satisfaction and to the court's satisfaction the matter of this hearing?"

"Yes, your Honor, and he is prepared."

"Does the prosecution have anything to add at this time?" the Judge asked, turning his attention to the County Attorney.

"No, your Honor, but we do wish to discuss the matter of bail when the time arrives."

"You will get that chance. Now, Mr. Diaz, would you approach the bench. You may have Mr. Stoner accompany you if you like."

"Thank you, your Honor, and I do wish that my attorney accompany me." Diaz replied.

"Mr. Joseph Carlos Diaz, do you understand the charges that have been filed against you and brought before this court."

"Yes, your Honor."

The judge read the complaint against Joseph Carlos Diaz. The complaint outlined the events of the crime and the apprehension of the suspect. "Now, Mr. Diaz, do you understand what I have read to you so far?"

"Yes, your Honor."

"Do you understand that this crime of burglary in the second degree carries with it a fine of up to $10,000 and a prison sentence of up to ten years."

"Yes, your Honor."

"Do you wish to enter a plea at this time?"

"I do, your Honor."

"And what is your plea, guilty or not guilty?"

"Not guilty, your Honor."

The Judge accepted the plea and continued "Now for the matter of bail. Does the prosecution wish to add anything at this time before I set bail?"

"We ask that the court delay setting bail until later this afternoon. Our office is right now in the process of issuing an arrest warrant for murder in the second degree against Mr. Diaz. Given the importance of the fact that Mr. Diaz is living out of a hotel room in Minneapolis and that his permanent residence is out of state, we ask that he be remanded back to the custody of the Sheriff and held in jail without bail until the murder warrant is issued and his arraignment for that offense is held."

"Does the defense have anything to say at this time?"

"Yes, your Honor. This hearing is only for the charge of burglary and nothing else. What transpires at a later date is of no significance to this hearing. My client is a professional person, a psychologist. He has had no other prior convictions, not even a traffic ticket. He is married and poses no threat to society. He has assured me that he will stay in the area until this whole matter is settled."

"I am going to honor the wishes of the prosecution at this time and set a future time for setting bail. It may be as early as this afternoon or as late as the day after tomorrow. Court is adjourned."

On the advice of his attorney, Joe Diaz appeared in front of the Judge wearing a suit, tie, and was neatly groomed and clean-shaven. He looked out of place in the leather shackles on his ankles and the handcuffs that were placed through a restraining belt around his waist. After he was manacled, the two deputies rushed him out of the side entrance of the courthouse and down the elevator to an awaiting squad car.

The courtroom was packed with onlookers and a larger crowd was gathered outside the courthouse. Many of them were waiting at the rear exit of the courthouse where Diaz would be brought out and put into a waiting squad car before being returned to the Law Enforcement Center. The crowd outside was angry and unruly. They had heard all the rumors and were convinced of Diaz' guilt. They would take the law into their own hands if need be but Diaz wasn't going to get off killing seven people in their county. Most of the agitators were from the Twin Cities and were only there for the chance to cause some disruption against the establishment. There were maybe a dozen locals in the gathering and most of them were quiet, peaceful, and curious. They wanted to get a closer look at the man who was rumored to have killed their own. Captain Bartholomew was walking through the crowd, agitating them as he promised he would when he left the Sheriff's office. His presence made the situation worse. If Joe Diaz were alone right now, they might have severely injured him or even killed him. Many in the crowd carried placards which read 'LET'S HAVE OUR SECOND HANGING'. Some read 'MURDERER' or 'DIE'. Most of the placards though read simply '1898/1994'. As one of the deputies was putting Diaz in the back seat of the squad car, he carefully scanned the area for possible trouble. "What do those signs mean?" he asked the other deputy, pointing to the white cardboard sign which read '1898/1994'.

"It's got something to do with a hanging here at the courthouse in 1898 and I guess they want another one now."

Joe Diaz was escorted safely back to the law enforcement center where he was unshackled and placed in the attorney's room to wait for Ivan Stoner.

Josh Trimble stuck his head into the Sheriff's office, "Got the results back from the lab on the evidence from our search of the Diaz car and hotel room."

The Sheriff was reading the Bishop Gazette when Josh entered the room and neatly laid it on his desk as he listened to him tell of the search warrant results "Good news, I hope," the Sheriff replied, hoping for a positive answer.

"Not so good on the calligraphy set. The inks in the set do not match any of the ink used on the calling cards and the pens don't match either. But, yes, I do have some good news. The blood type on the knife we found in the trunk of Diaz' car matches the blood type of Sylvia Pennington. We were able to lift one print off the knife and it matches Diaz."

"So we got him?"

"Yea, I think we do. I have given the lab report to the County Attorney to add to the warrant. We'll have to let Stoner know as soon as possible. I don't know if Diaz realizes we searched his room yet, but he is going to find out in a hell of a hurry once Stoner finds out." The Agent turned to walk out of the Sheriff's office when he stopped, remembering another reason why he was there. "I just got off the phone with Odell and he tells me Tommy is coming back to their house today. He says he is back to normal but they don't want us talking to him until after the weekend. They want some time with him alone to get reacquainted."

"Great," the Sheriff answered, lifting his head up from the newspaper he had returned to. "Let's hope he is able to identify the person that killed his family."

"I hope he is ready for my questions and doesn't slip back to the catatonic state he was in. I'd feel terrible. But Odell assured me that the psychiatrist gave him a complete bill of health. He is back to where he was before the murders and is functioning very well. If he picks out Diaz in those videos as the murderer, we've got ourselves more than enough probable cause. I would say we got a pretty solid case."

Josh moved from the doorway to a chair and sat down. "I know it seems silly, but I am still not convinced Diaz did it. If Tommy picks him out, I'll feel better."

"What are you talking about, Josh?" the Sheriff asked, perplexed at Josh's uncertainty.

"It just bothers me that I cannot find a motive. With murders like these, the killer has to have a reason for doing what he did. There's got to be a motive, I just need to find it. I'd feel better if I knew what it was, that's all."

"Do you think he did it?"

"Right now, I'm not sure. But with the evidence we have, I would have to say there is a good chance."

"Odell must have contacted the Bishop Gazette before he let us know, or else the Gazette found it out on their own, but look at this," the Sheriff said as he handed the newspaper to Josh.

Josh noticed the headlines of the paper:

TOMMY HELMS COMES HOME

A team of psychiatrists at the Mayo Clinic, headed by Dr. Lebowitz, have been working with Tommy Helms for the past four months. Tommy was in an almost semi-catatonic state when he first arrived at the Mayo Clinic. Yesterday, he was pronounced 100% cured and will be returning to Bishop today. Tommy was the only survivor of the massacre that took place at his home last November. His mother and his two sisters were killed in that incident.

Law enforcement authorities in Davis County, along with the State Bureau of Criminal Apprehension, are hoping that Tommy can identify the killer. A suspect in the case, Joe Diaz, will be charged with second-degree murder sometime within the next 36 hours.

Eight year old Tommy Helms is staying with his grandparents, Odell and Betty Graban of Bishop. They say they are anxious to have Tommy back.

After reading the story, Josh handed the newspaper back to the Sheriff. *Where did they get their information? It's yellow journalism and disgusting reporting.* "You're going to have to furnish protection for the kid."

"What do you mean?"

"What if Diaz isn't the killer? If he's not, then the real killer will try and get to Tommy as soon as possible to shut him up. The damn paper even said where he would be staying!"

"You are really not sure about Diaz, are you?"

"Cautious is all. There is more to this case than what we know," Josh reiterated his suggestion to the Sheriff, but it had now become more of a demand. "Please tell me that you will give Tommy protection. I'm serious. He could be in real danger. I think you should have two guards at the Graban house all the time."

The Sheriff relented and ordered Deputy Blume to his office.

"What can I do for you, Sheriff?" his Chief Deputy asked as he walked into the office.

"You do know that the Helms boy is coming back to Bishop and he is staying at the Grabans."

"Yea, everybody in town knows. It's plastered all over the Gazette," Frank answered.

"Josh here thinks we should give Tommy some protection until he at least identifies the murderer. Josh has a good point. If Diaz isn't the killer, the real killer may try and get to him. You're going to have to use our reserve deputies on this. I can't spare any more of my men right now."

"I'll get right on it," Deputy Blume answered.

At four o'clock in the afternoon, a murder warrant was issued and served on the prisoner, Joe Diaz, who was in the attorney's room talking to Ivan Stoner when he received it. Ivan Stoner spent several hours with his client before he contacted the jailor to let him out.

- 22 -

Alter ego - regarded as that other second self

an inseparable friend

[Lat: other self]

Webster's Dictionary of the English Language

Jim Bowden, Davis County Attorney, telephoned Sheriff Bean at his office in the Law Enforcement Center informing him that a meeting was going to be held in his office at nine-thirty and that he wanted the Sheriff and Trimble to attend. The Sheriff looked at his watch; it was a few minutes past eight. "We'll be there; I'll call Josh and let him know. What's this all about?"

"Ivan Stoner requested it; he wants you to bring Diaz. He says he has some information that will prove his client is innocent of any murders," the County Attorney replied.

Ivan Stoner and County Attorney Jim Bowden were waiting in the conference room when the Sheriff, Agent Trimble, and their handcuffed prisoner, Joe Diaz, arrived. The Sheriff entered the room first, followed by Diaz, and then by Josh Trimble. After the conference room door was closed, the Sheriff unfastened the handcuffs from the wrists of Diaz and put the handcuffs in a leather case that was attached to his belt. He was not in leg irons today. His behavior over the last few days had earned him some trust with the Sheriff and Bean felt the extra shackles were unnecessary. Diaz looked around the familiar setting of the conference room. As a psychologist, he'd had many meetings with attorneys and the decor was similar. Attorneys had no imagination. This conference room was no different. Huge bookcases stood against the wall on all four sides of the room holding volumes of law books. In the center of the carpeted room was positioned an elongated dark stained oak table with several red leather chairs strategically placed around it. A bust of the Roman orator Cicero stood on top of one of the bookcases and a picture of Abraham Lincoln seated in a chair hung between two smaller bookcases on one of the walls. After everyone was seated, Jim Bowden started the meeting by informing Josh and the Sheriff that Ivan called him last night and told him of his latest conversation with his client. "After we are through, Ivan wants to suggest a plea bargain agreement for us to consider. I'm going to let Mr. Stoner begin, but first I am going to have my stenographer come in and take notes of this meeting." Bowden contacted his secretary through his intercom and the legal secretary entered and took a seat at one end of the table. After she was seated, he turned the meeting over to Ivan Stoner.

"Thank you, Jim. First of all, let me tell you that I spent four hours last night with Mr. Diaz. The story he told me was absolutely incredible and that's why we're here today. His unusual story will clear him of any implication in these murders, as you will soon discover. I am going to have Mr. Diaz do the talking and I don't feel that I will have to interrupt him at all, but I want you to feel free to stop him at any time if you have questions," he said, glancing at Sheriff Bean and then Agent Trimble. "Is there anything you two would like to say before we get started?"

Both Sheriff Bean and Josh nodded in the negative, anxious to hear what Diaz was about to say. Stoner turned the meeting over to his client and once again urged that either Bean or Trimble should feel free to interrupt at any time.

"First of all, I am not your killer," Diaz began and then hesitated, waiting for a reaction from either Trimble or the Sheriff or the County Attorney.

The Sheriff quickly answered "gee, where have I heard that before, suppose you tell us who it is."

Unshaken by the Sheriff's sarcasm he began, "Your killer is Pastor Bartholomew. I have been tracking him for the last year and a half trying to get enough evidence to convince myself and the authorities that he was the killer. As you know, I am from Ypsilanti, Michigan and so is the Pastor."

"We didn't know he was from Michigan but that town has been popping up a lot lately." the Sheriff interrupted. "To be honest with you, he never was a suspect so we don't know much about the guy."

"I realize that and this is why I want to fill you in on him. A little over a year ago my daughter was murdered just outside Ypsilanti. She was living in a little town about four miles away from our home. She was living with her boyfriend at the time. He worked mostly nights so she spent a lot of evenings at home alone. On the night of Good Friday, he had to work a twelve-hour shift to cover for another person who wanted the Easter weekend off. He didn't get home until Saturday morning at around eight. He found her on the living room couch with her throat slit and her hair cut off. The authorities could not find any evidence except for a few prints that were made by bedroom slippers or sandals. I now know it was sandals and I will tell you why later. The sandals had traces of my daughter's blood on them but they were unable to trace the shoe prints. That was the only piece of evidence they had. The case is still open and unsolved and they still haven't found a motive. In that area, two more women were murdered in the same ritualistic manner.   These other two murders happened between Thanksgiving and Easter. Again, the authorities uncovered very little evidence, not enough to go on anyway. So we now had three women murdered, all killed the same way, and all unsolved. Here's where the pastor comes in. All three women belonged to the Abundant Life Church in Ypsilanti. And guess what, Pastor Bartholomew was the pastor at that church. Now this church that the pastor was head of wasn't very big. Unlike Bishop, the Abundant Life Church in Ypsilanti had only one hundred and fifty members. So what are the odds of three members of this congregation being murdered first of all, and then all killed the same way. That tells me that someone in that church knew the victims and killed them. It wasn't only my daughter who belonged the church but our whole family, so I knew almost everybody in the church and none of them were suspects to me. I always thought the pastor was kind of an odd duck so I concentrated my efforts on him initially. When I started finding out how strange he was I knew I had the killer but needed to prove it."

"Did the killer leave any kind of calling card at these murders?" the Sheriff asked.

"No, but I know what you are getting at. I had heard there were calling cards left at each murder around here. None were left at the murders in Ypsilanti."

"How did you know there were calling cards left at our murder scenes?" Josh asked curiously, as he was frantically writing down everything that the suspect was saying.

"I have my ways. I have learned a lot of investigative techniques since I have been chasing Bartholomew. I don't know what the cards read but I do know that they were left."

"Let me interrupt for a second," Stoner intervened. "Mr. Diaz is not aware of all the facts that you have on the case. We didn't talk much about your evidence because I spent the four hours last night listening to Mr. Diaz's story and didn't have time to go into much more. If he seems somewhat naive about your evidence that's why."

"Does the word "dooble" mean anything to you?" Josh asked.

Diaz rolled his eyes a couple of times toward the ceiling, trying to recall the significance of the name. In a very short time, less than thirty seconds, it had come to him. When it did, a slight smile appeared on his face. "That was the nickname of Bartholomew when he was in grade school and even into his first couple of years of high school. He got it in the fourth grade and had to live with the name until at least the tenth grade. He hated that name and the more he made it known he hated it, the worse the name calling got. In fact, if you want, I can tell you how he got it."

"Go ahead," Josh said, realizing this part of the puzzle that had been baffling him so much may be solved.

"I learned this by talking to his fourth grade teacher who still remembers the incident and also Bartholomew. Well, to go on, there was a class in spelling and each student had to go up front and spell the word on the chalkboard that the teacher gave them. The whole class was allowed to watch, and if a mistake was made, the class would laugh at the speller. It was Bartholomew's turn and his word to spell was 'double'. You guessed it; he walked up to the chalkboard and wrote 'dooble'. Well the class laughed uproariously at this and Bartholomew was so embarrassed he ran out of the classroom and went immediately home. He didn't show up at school for three days. When he finally came back, everyone in the school started calling him 'dooble'."

"Either you know about the calling cards left at the scene and you are the killer, or you honestly don't know, so I'll fill you in and maybe you can tell me the significance of the cards," Josh said explaining to Diaz about each card left at the crime scene and what it had said. Josh was also fishing for any holes in his story to solidify their case against him. Stoner had already agreed that anything said in the meeting could be used in Court and he wouldn't object.

"As a psychologist, I have spent many years studying human behavior. Bartholomew is one of the strangest I have run across. It is my professional opinion that the use of those cards and then the final card on the Pennington murder was his way of cleansing himself of that name forever. Not only did he finally get rid of that nickname but he was helping his vengeful God in purging the world of sin. There were seven murders and in the Bible; 'seven' represents completion."

"Let me get this straight. Are you telling me that Bartholomew thought he was doing God's work by killing these people?" the Sheriff asked, appearing a little bewildered by what he was hearing. "You mean he could kill two little girls and an old lady and that was God's work?"

"That's right," Diaz said. "I'll give you the reason for each killing if you want."

"I would appreciate that. Let's start with the Helm's murders," the Sheriff said and then added. "Also, while you are at it, you might want to tell us why you were there burglarizing the place."

"First of all, Sheriff, I'm certain you know that each murder happened around a holiday," Diaz stated, looking at the Sheriff, with the Sheriff nodding that he was aware of it. "Well, each of the murders in Ypsilanti happened within a couple of days preceding a holiday. We have the same situation here. The exception is the Helm's murder which happened after October 31. That, as you know, is Halloween, but it is also the day before All Saints Day. I believe Bartholomew would have murdered the Helm's family on the thirtieth but he forgot that he was leaving for the cities that night and wouldn't return until the afternoon of the thirty-first so he decided to kill them on Halloween night. The Halloween storm messed him up also and now he couldn't get to their house until a day after the storm and the roads were partially opened. Nothing, not even his murder plans got in the way of his secret jaunts to Minneapolis."

"What's the significance of the holidays?" Josh asked.

"All Saints Day, Christmas and Easter are church holidays and Thanksgiving isn't but is recognized as kind of a church holiday by some people. He killed them as a sacrifice to his God, believing he was purging the world of yet one more sinner and what a better time to do it than on a church holiday." Diaz stopped for a second and asked for a glass of water. The secretary who had been frantically taking notes got up, returned shortly with an empty glass and a pitcher of water, and set it down in front of Diaz. He poured himself a glass, took a large gulp and continued. "Please realize, gentlemen, that what I am telling you is conjecture only but with my experience in the field of psychology, and my intense study of this man, I feel I am real close in my analysis of his personality. That aside though, let me continue with the Helms case. Mary Helms was divorced and this was a big 'NO' for the pastor. Not only was she divorced but she was sleeping around with one of your deputies. She was now a harlot in his eyes and a woman that was corrupting the morals of other people. As a member of his church, she had to go. The two daughters had to be killed too because they were going to be a product of her sinful living. You know, the sins of the mother will be passed onto the daughters, or something like that. Anyway, if the daughters were allowed to live, they would grow up and be just like their mother and would corrupt the world just as Mary Helms' had. You see, gentlemen, this is what we are dealing with."

"Amazing," Jim Bowden spoke out loud, without realizing it.

"What about Mattie Blake? Here was a regular church goer, a member of the congregation for years, a hard worker in the church, and a friend of the pastor," the Sheriff asked, a little afraid to hear the answer.

"Her murder confused me too, but I did a lot of interviewing with her friends and family. I found out some things that would lead me to understand why she was killed. You're right about her devotion to the church, but she and the pastor weren't that good of friends. She had confided in a few people, especially her daughter, that she thought the pastor was very strange and that she was even afraid of him. She thought she was the only one in the congregation who felt this way because no one else ever mentioned having those kind of feelings. Everybody in the church seemed to be satisfied with the job he was doing. It bothered her a lot and she began looking for another church. At the same time this was going on, a Jehovah Witness came to her house and talked to her. She eventually planned on joining that church and had told Bartholomew about it. Bartholomew hated the Jehovah Witnesses and thought anybody that belonged to that 'cult' was doomed to hell. He also didn't like the idea that the Witnesses were now going to get some of Mattie's money instead of his church, the true church, the church that needed it more than the damn Jehovah Witnesses. She had to be killed while her soul could still be saved. The church was to be left a sizeable amount from the estate so the time was ripe for the murder."

"We did a thorough check on Mattie Blake's background and talked to all her friends and family for some clue as to why she was killed. We did everything you did, so why do you have so much more than we do?" the Sheriff asked, perplexed and feeling a little dismayed that they weren't able to get more evidence.

"Don't feel bad, Sheriff. We were both looking for different things so we were asking different questions. I knew who the killer was, you didn't. It's as simple as that."

"You might as well give us your theories on the murders of the Anderson and Rawlings girls too," the Sheriff asked, now starting to believe what Diaz was saying and remembering that Josh never was sure about Diaz being the murderer.

"That relationship may have been more than just being friends and I think the pastor knew it. Of course, that being the case, our twisted pastor decided they were the worst kind of sinners. He must have followed them around a lot though, to know that they would be parked in a gravel pit. He liked to do his killing in homes. I don't know why he killed them in a gravel pit and I don't know why the girls were there. Maybe he thought their apartment was too dangerous of a place to kill them; too many nosy tenants and the walls were paper thin. It definitely wasn't a part of his pattern but by now his mind is deteriorating at a faster rate and he thinks he is God's judge and jury. Even though he is getting loonier, he is still very cunning and very clever. I know you think this is getting weird but, believe me, it gets weirder."

"When this whole thing gets settled, Diaz, I want to know where you are getting some of your information," the Sheriff stated.

"Mr. Diaz," Josh began after the Sheriff was done. "The final murder intrigues me the most. Is this his last murder? Why was Sylvia Pennington murdered? She didn't belong to the church."

"I can't shed much light on that one yet. You see, I've been in jail since the murder and haven't had a whole lot of time to work on the case. I don't know if this is the last murder or not because the bastard is getting crazier and crazier as time goes on. Tell me a little about the case and maybe I can steer you in the right direction."

Josh briefly explained the murder and the information they had so far.

"First, you say she was recently divorced, that fits. Now you should check on her husband and see if he belonged to the Abundant Life Church. I'll bet he does and I'll bet he knows Bartholomew pretty well. Sorry I can't be much help on this case but I think you understand why."

Ivan held up his hand indicating to his client that he should stop talking. He looked at the Sheriff and Josh hoping to read their thoughts. "I believe his story and I hope that in the end, you will too. I wouldn't have asked for this meeting if I thought he was lying to me." Ivan Stoner couldn't get a read on what either of the men were thinking so he motioned for his client to continue.

Josh asked the County Attorney if he could smoke in his office. Bowden reluctantly said "Go ahead; there's an ashtray on the table behind you. I really don't like smoking in this room but I know that Ivan here is going to light up one of his damn cigars anytime now so a little cigarette smoke ain't going to hurt nothing."

Ivan looked at Josh, winked and pulled out a cigar from his jacket pocket and lit it. He turned to Diaz and told him to continue.

"You know the pastor is gay?" Diaz said and looked directly at the Sheriff and Trimble for a response. When there was none, he began, "I first realized he was gay when I began tailing him everywhere he went. Mondays were his days off in Ypsilanti so on Sunday evening he would head for a gay bar. We had a couple in Ypsilanti so he didn't have far to drive. Anyway, he would frequent one of the bars around eight o'clock in the evening and at eleven or so he would walk out with another man and they would head for a motel and spend the night. In the morning, Bartholomew would treat the man to breakfast at a nearby restaurant. The two men would say their 'goodbyes' and then Bartholomew would return home. This went on week after week and it must have cost him a pretty penny and to this day I don't know where he gets all his money. He was paying a hundred dollars for a male prostitute, another sixty for a motel room, and breakfast the next morning. At first I didn't realize he was paying for the services of another man until I began checking around. I went into these gay bars and asked about the pastor and was told he was paying for sex and would try and choose a different partner each time. His routine was the same in Minneapolis except he had Wednesdays off here so he left for the cities on Tuesday evening and returned late Wednesday evening."

"I personally have nothing against the gay lifestyle and have counseled many gays in my career as a psychologist. Even though I personally want to kill this guy, it has nothing to do with his sexual orientation. In fact, even though I can't stand the bastard, his homosexuality may have contributed to why he is the way he is. I feel a lot of sympathy with what he had to go through growing up. Imagine the troubles he must have had. First of all he grew up in a small mid-western town, a staunchly conservative Midwest town. He realizes he is gay at about the age of fifteen or sixteen. He has to keep it hidden and doesn't understand his sexuality yet at that age but he knows he is different from the other boys in his class. Can you imagine being gay and hearing all the gay jokes going around the school? At that time there was a lot of gay bashing and the jokes about the queers and the faggots must have had a great effect on him. He knew he was one and this made it worse. He wouldn't dare tell anyone for fear that he would get beaten up or maybe even killed. On top of that, his father was the all-American father. He loved sports and played football, basketball, and baseball in college. He was a fisherman and a hunter. He was everything that Bartholomew wasn't. He loved his son deeply but noticed that his son was growing away from him. He couldn't understand his son. The poor kid was short, skinny, had fair skin and loved music, art and books. He took no interest in any kind of sports. The father and son were opposites and so grew apart. This also hurt him and he started retreating into himself. He became a loner. So now he had his homosexuality to deal with, the kids at school to deal with, and his father who he felt didn't love him any more because he was who he was. At this point in his life, he really didn't like who he was. After graduating from high school, he applied and was accepted at Notre Dame. He decided at that time he wanted to be a priest. He left the Catholic Church after he graduated from college and joined the Abundant Life Church. It was in college that the real transformation of Bartholomew took place. In his freshman year, he joined the ROTC and adapted quickly to the military lifestyle. He loved it and became obsessed with its order, discipline, and regiment. That is when his alter ego developed. He was now two people. He was the passive gay pastor and also the aggressive all American male who believe in God, country, and apple pie. The two egos are now friends; they are like brothers to each other. The pastor accepted things as they were and talked about them to his alter ego. If the pastor was wronged, the alter ego then did what had to be done to protect his passive friend. An example would be Mattie Blake. My guess is that she went to his office and told him she was leaving the church and taking her money with her. He, of course, being the passive one, accepted this but tried to convince her to stay in the church. I'm sure he tried to convince her also that the Jehovah Witnesses were nothing more than a cult. Apparently he couldn't persuade her and she was firm in her decision. Now he is feeling bad about Mattie Blake. She was a good church worker and had a lot of friends in the church. She might even try to convince other members to leave the church. She was removing the church from her will; money that the church needed. Well, the pastor discusses this with his alter ego and the alter ego decides to take matters into his own hands. He is going to kill Mattie. This way the church will get its share of the will, Mattie will be buried through the church, and no one will know that she had decided to leave it. As you can see, each murder was done to protect the pastor or the church. Most of the murders were done to cleanse the church of sinners."

"Why don't you stop there, Joe. We've covered a lot so far. Do either you or Josh have any questions for Mr. Diaz?" Stoner said looking at the Sheriff, then at Josh.

The Sheriff motioned to Ivan Stoner that he did have a question and looked at the defendant still not convinced of his innocence or guilt. The Sheriff started, "Did you know that the pastor's brother came to my office dressed in his uniform and told me you confessed to the crimes?"

"The Pastor doesn't have a brother; Pastor Bartholomew and Captain Bartholomew are the same person. I'm not surprised he came to your office. He has got to be feeling that you are getting close to solving this case and he is worried that he may be found out. What did he tell you?"

The Sheriff and Josh both sat straight up in their comfortable chairs when they heard that the Captain and the Pastor were one in the same. Josh looked at the Sheriff and then at Joe Diaz. "We thought Captain Bartholomew was the pastor's real brother. They do look a lot alike but the Captain had light brown hair and a darker complexion. He also wasn't wearing glasses. He had us fooled."

"He was pretty good at disguises; he was pulling off this masquerade for many years. He got real good at it. What did he come to your office for?" Diaz asked.

"He told me that on the night of the Mattie Blake funeral you came to his office and confessed. He said you handed over to him the murder weapon which happened to be an army issue knife. He said he told you that he would not turn you in if you didn't commit any more murders. After the Pennington murder, he realized you were not going to stop the killings and that is why he had his brother come to see me."

"I never went to visit the pastor and I can't prove my whereabouts at that time," Diaz replied. "I never owned an army knife in my life. Was it the murder weapon?"

"The knife wounds on the first six victims were consistent with the measurements of the knife he gave us," Josh replied.

"Of course, you realize he would have easy access to an army knife," Diaz pointed out.

"Yes," Josh answered.

"Can you tell us anything about his years at Notre Dame? Were there any incidents at the college while he was there?" the Sheriff asked.

"Yes there were, but nothing that could be linked to him. There were eleven violent non-sexual assaults against females while he was attending Notre Dame. My guess is he was involved in these but I have no proof."

"You say there were three murders of church members at your church. Were there any other churches he was a pastor at and did they have any incidents?" Josh asked.

"He was a pastor at two other churches and they didn't have any problems. I don't know if he was able to suppress his alter ego at that time or if there was no reason to commit murder in these congregations. I do know he was having a hard time with some of the members of his congregation in Ypsilanti and there were a few that wanted to give him the boot. I think the pressure there might have brought the alter ego out and he became more violent at this time."

"Mr. Diaz, we did a search of your hotel room in Minneapolis and found a calligraphy set. Now here are the many coincidences we are dealing with and why you were charged with murder. I don't know if you know this but each calling card left at the death scenes was done in calligraphy. How do you explain that?" Josh asked, reaching for another cigarette. The room was a hazy blue by now with the cigar smoke from Ivan Stoner's huge stogie. One more cigarette wasn't going to affect the air any worse than what it was.

Diaz seemed surprised that his room was searched and then remembered that Ivan had given him the search warrant to look over but that had gotten sidetracked when they started talking about the pastor. "I heard about the calling cards he was leaving at the crime scenes so I bought a calligraphy set in Minneapolis and decided that I would let him know that someone was on to him. I took a six-hour course at the University of Minnesota on calligraphy and had become pretty good at it when I started writing short letters to Bartholomew. You see, I was trying to make his life as miserable as I could. I was trying to drive him over the edge and at the same time was plotting to kill him. I wanted revenge for the death of my daughter and I didn't want any more people killed. I know that you don't have the death penalty here in Minnesota so I was going to at least be his emotional death penalty. Well anyway, after each murder, I would burglarize his office at the church. I mean I tore everything apart. I threw books all over the floor, emptied out his desk on the floor, and ripped everything off the wall. Then I left my little note which read in calligraphy 'You killed my daughter and now I am going to kill you.' I also had another reason for tearing his office apart. I was searching for a gold necklace with a gold cross on it. It was my daughter's and it was ripped off her neck when she was murdered and never found. I was looking for that necklace and when I found it, I would have enough evidence to either go to the police or take the law into my on hands. I also burglarized his house several times. I noticed he never reported any of the burglaries because he didn't want any suspicion brought upon him. That's why I had the calligraphy set, just to mess with him."

"The most damaging evidence we have against you is your hunting knife we found in your trunk. The blood on that knife is the same blood type as Sylvia Pennington's. Not only that, the measurements on this knife are consistent with the wounds on the victim. We also found traces of paper towel on the knife. I imagine someone tried to wipe the knife clean with it. Do you own a hunting knife and where is it now?"

Diaz once again looked surprised as he glanced at his attorney for some signal or eye contact that would indicate that everything was okay. "Yes, I own a hunting knife and I keep it in the trunk of the rental car. I can't explain how it got blood on it because it was always in my possession. What did this knife look like?"

"The blade was seven inches long and it had an ivory handle with a narrow strip of inlaid silver," Josh answered.

"That's not my knife. The knife I own has a shorter blade and a wooden handle. It is just a cheap hunting knife. I had planned on using it on Bartholomew when the time was right. He must have switched knives on me. Where was my car when you guys did the search?"

"It was locked and in our impound yard which is also locked," the Sheriff answered.

"Bartholomew must have switched knives. He had to have been on to who I was and now he had his chance to nail me and take all the suspicion off him. Bartholomew learned locksmithing in the Army and simply used his skills to get into the impound lot and my trunk. Do you ever have any guards posted at the impound lot?"

"No," the Sheriff answered, realizing that Diaz seemed to have an answer for everything. "How do you explain the fact that we lifted one of your fingerprints off the knife?"

"I don't know." Diaz said trying to think of a reasonable explanation as to why his print would be on a knife he had never seen. His facial expression turned from one of thoughtfulness to one of elation when he remembered what took place between him and Deputy Crawford. "I got it! A couple of hours after I was booked, I had asked Deputy Crawford if I could go to my car and get some of my toiletries out of the trunk. The deputy informed me that my car was in an impound lot and that he couldn't take me. I kept begging him because I was getting real grubby looking and he finally relented. He and a jailor took me to my car at around five in the morning and we were back in less than fifteen minutes. I must have touched the knife accidentally. Thinking it was my knife, any way, I thought nothing of it. It was dark where the car was parked and I could only grope inside the trunk until I found what I wanted. That's the only time it could have happened. The pastor is known to drive around at all hours of the night. He had just killed someone earlier that evening and still had the murder weapon in the car. He must have seen my car parked there and didn't realize what was all going on. My guess is that he parked somewhere near the impound lot, got the gate open, found my car and opened the trunk. He must have noticed there was a knife lying on the floor of the trunk so he simply switched knives. This was his chance to nail me for the murders he had committed. He knew what kind of car I was driving because he watched me get into it after Mattie Blake's funeral."

"I can verify that, Sheriff. Bones told me about it the next morning," Josh said, informing the Sheriff the incident did happen.

Paul Daffinrud

"What were you doing in the Helms house when our deputies caught you?" the Sheriff asked.

"Just looking for evidence you might have overlooked. The house had been vacant since the murders so nothing had been moved. I know it was a long shot, but I was searching for anything I could find. I just needed more evidence to put my case together, that's all. I didn't think anybody would be up at that hour and see me pull into the driveway. When I was arrested, it was the scariest experience of my life."

The Sheriff went on, "When you were staying at the Holiday Inn in Cedarton, you would leave your hotel room at about midnight and drive around until at least two thirty in the morning. Why were you doing this?"

"I was trying to catch Bartholomew out and about at that time of night. He usually killed between those hours and I wanted to follow him and hoped to prevent another killing."

"Why were you gone for three months and then return to another killing here in Bishop?" Josh asked.

"I had become familiar with Bartholomew's pattern and I was pretty confident he wouldn't kill again until the Easter holidays. I felt it was safe to leave for a while and I wanted to be with my wife and children. I missed them after not seeing them for so long."

Josh was twirling his pencil between his index finger and middle finger studying his notes. Satisfied that he had written down everything that was covered so far, he looked up at Diaz and said, "the sandals." Diaz looked at Josh, waiting for more. "The sandals," he repeated, more like he was thinking out loud than asking a question. "You said there were shoe prints left at the scene of your daughter's murder and that it was possible that those prints were from a bedroom slipper or sandal. We had similar prints left at our murder scenes. What's your theory on that?"

"Personally," Diaz began, "I feel that he wore his army fatigues at each of the killings and instead of combat boots, he wore sandals. I believe that Bartholomew killed both as the pastor and as the captain. It's like the captain did the killings but the pastor came along as a friend to help. As the captain, he was very meticulous about not leaving any evidence at the crime scene but, as the pastor, he was more careless, leaving shoe prints at almost every scene." Diaz finished, hoping what he was saying made sense. "Please realize that I have theorized most of what I have told you today. I am basing these theories on my education and my years of experience. It is possible I may be wrong on some things, but I am sure that I am about as close as anybody can get. I have chased Bartholomew and studied his behavior too long to not feel that I am close to the truth."

Josh studied his notes, and then looked at Diaz. "I have one more question; you mentioned that your daughter had her hair cut off. Every one of our victims also had their hair cut off. We could never understand why, it made no sense to us."

"Bartholomew did not like himself very well. He didn't like what he had become and he didn't like the way he looked and he didn't like being short. He's got this mirror in his office that reflects his image to be somewhat larger than he is. I can picture him standing in front of that mirror visualizing himself as someone quite different. His hair was thinning and turning gray at the same time. I know this caused him great consternation and he felt shamed by his appearance and his balding head of hair. Cutting off his victim's hair brought them down to his level. In his mind, his shame transferred to his victims." Diaz finished his explanation and poured himself a glass of water. "Is there anything else?"

The room fell silent as the information was being digested. Jim Bowden looked at the Sheriff who motioned he had no more questions. He then turned to Josh who indicated the same. The County Attorney faced Ivan Stoner who had the hint of a smile on his lips. "Do we have your permission to talk to Mr. Diaz if we think of anything else?"

"No, you don't. I have talked with Mr. Diaz about that and we both agree that I should be present at all interrogations or meetings you have with him. After all, he is still in your custody and has these charges hanging over his head. For now though, I think you should have Mr. Diaz taken back to the jail and we should talk about what we have just heard. Do you all agree?"

Everyone agreed and Jim Bowden looked at his watch. "It's quarter to twelve, why don't we go out and have some lunch together and then return here." The Sheriff called his office and made arrangements to have Diaz transported back to jail. After Diaz was gone, Ivan Stoner suggested they walk over to the Torchlight Restaurant for lunch and discuss the details of the case as they had developed so far.

- 23 -

The Torchlight Restaurant was the more upscale of the two restaurants in town. It was here that the business people took their noon lunches and the Rotary Club, the Lions Club, and the Chamber of Commerce all met for their weekly or monthly meetings. Unlike the Bishop Cafe, the Torchlight was carpeted, muffling the noise of the crowd. The walls were paneled in dark mahogany and each wall was adorned with several Norman Rockwell paintings. A stone fountain stood in the middle of the restaurant but hadn't worked for years and was now used by the waitresses to set their trays on while they passed around plates of food to their customers. A small bar with hundreds of colorful liquor decanters lining its shelves was hidden from the main part of the restaurant but was available if anyone wanted a drink with their meal.

Ivan Stoner, who was partial to having a couple of Scotch Manhattans with his lunch, favored eating at the Torchlight over the Bishop Cafe which didn't serve alcohol. He had become a more frequent visitor to the Torchlight of late now that he was dating the manager of the restaurant. Ivan pulled his cell phone from his briefcase and called the Torchlight Restaurant and made a reservation for four. When they arrived, they were escorted to their table by Diane, the manager. She took their orders and brought Ivan his Scotch Manhattan. No one else at the booth wanted a drink, but Ivan was used to that by now. He sometimes yearned for the good old days when people actually had a couple of drinks with their noon meal. *Was he the only holdout left in this politically correct world?* Ivan took a sip from his drink and gently placed it on the napkin that accompanied his Manhattan. "Well, what you think about Mr. Diaz after this morning?" he asked, aware that he had developed a slight turmoil for the prosecution's case.

"I don't know, Ivan. His story seems plausible enough and maybe he is telling us the truth, but we've got to check the facts out first," the Sheriff answered.

"Well, I'll tell you this. I am convinced he is telling the truth. I certainly wouldn't blow my whole defense strategy in court by allowing this meeting if I wasn't sure," Stoner replied.

"We're going to know the identity of the killer after Monday any way so I think we should hold off until then before anything is decided upon," Josh stated.

"You talking about the Helms kid, Josh? Do you think he can identify the killer?" Ivan asked.

"I'm certain of it. He created too much of a ruckus after watching the funeral of his mother and sisters to not know who it was," Josh said.

"I've heard that story, but what if he had a memory loss after all this time? I mean, he went through a lot at the Mayo Clinic.

Maybe they were able to erase the events of that night from his mind," Ivan said with a feeling of uncertainty about Tommy's ability to pick out the killer.

"It's a chance I've got to take, but I feel confident that he will be able to pick out the killer of his mother and sisters," Josh replied.

"You talked about a plea agreement on this case. What did you have in mind, Ivan?" Bowden asked.

"Simply this. If my client is telling the truth, which I think he is, the murder charge would, of course, be dropped. But I also want the burglary charged dropped so he can leave here with a clean record. I mean his testimony this morning gives you enough to arrest Bartholomew and enough evidence to convict him," Ivan stated as if he were arguing the case in front of a judge.

"We don't know that he is telling us the truth, though, Ivan. Let's say that he is and we can get a warrant for Bartholomew because of it. I will consider dropping the burglary charge. I am still going to have to charge him with something. I mean he was in the house illegally and that is a crime. Maybe we could go with a misdemeanor trespass charge and a small fine. I can recommend to the court that his record be vindicated after a year if there are no more offenses in Minnesota," Bowden answered. The group had finished their meals and Bowden, the perpetual time watcher, looked at his watch and stated he had to get back to his office.

"We got to go too. There is a phone call I've got to make and do some ass chewing," the Sheriff said, just before taking his last sip of coffee.

The Sheriff was making small talk with Josh as they were walking out of the restaurant. He was holding the phone by his ear, waiting for an answer on the other end.

"Ypsilanti Police Department, how can I help you?" the female voice on the other end answered.

"This is Sheriff Milo Bean, Sheriff of Davis County in Minnesota. I need to talk to the sergeant on duty."

"Please hold," the dispatcher replied.

"Sergeant Peters," the voice on the other end said simply.

"Yes, Sergeant Peters, this is Sheriff Bean in Minnesota. Last November third, our office sent you a fax describing three murders which took place in our area. We asked your department, along with all other ones in the Midwest, to contact us if they had any murders similar to what we had. We received nothing from your office and now find out that a little over a year ago your department had three murders very similar to ours. I want to know why the hell you didn't answer us."

Sergeant Peters said he would check and put the Sheriff on hold. When he was back on the line, he told the Sheriff that they had no record of a fax like that coming through.

"That's a bunch of bullshit, Sergeant, because I have the copy of the fax in my office and it tells me that it was received by your office. I've got the date and time stamped on it."

"Maybe it got mislaid or lost in the shuffle," the sergeant answered, speaking more cautiously now that he sensed the man on the other end of the line was angry and probably had a right to be.

"I'm going to tell you something, Sergeant. If we had gotten a return call from you, we might not have had another four murders on our hands. That information from you would have been vital in our investigation. I don't know who messed up but I am going to write your Chief and let him know what happened. I hope somebody's ass gets hung out to dry over this. Goodbye," the Sheriff said, slamming shut the cell phone and returning it to his pocket. "Now that's incompetence," the Sheriff said, speaking to Josh, still angry with the phone conversation.

"Sheriff, I'm shocked. I don't see you get mad that often."

"Some things just piss you off. I was sure we would hear something back from one of the departments we had faxed. When we didn't, I thought our killer was someone who was from this area. If we had just heard from Ypsilanti immediately, we might have gone in the right direction on this case from the start. We wasted a lot of time for nothing and lost four more lives in the meantime. Damn right I'm mad."

"I hate to change the subject on you, Sheriff, but I called Odell. I'm going over to their home Monday morning to see Tommy. Did you want to come along?"

"No, you've dealt with the Grabans through this whole thing so why don't you go alone. I've got plenty of things to get caught up at the office. I wish you good luck though."

On Monday morning, DVDs in hand, Josh went to the Graban home. He was anxious, yet apprehensive, excited but cautious, optimistic and yet slightly pessimistic. Tommy held the key. He was the best evidence you could have, an eye witness. He hoped his feelings were correct and that Tommy could name the killer. He hoped that Ivan Stoner was wrong when he said the psychiatrists could have erased the memory of the traumatic experience from Tommy's mind.

Knocking on the door, he recognized the redolent smells of fresh coffee and cinnamon. Tommy opened the door and invited Josh in. He said his grandma and grandpa were waiting for him in the kitchen. Josh looked at Tommy and immediately noticed that Tommy's eyes were now a warm blue, so much different than the eyes that had reminded him of a darkness of the soul. His flesh was now a fresh pink color like little boys are supposed to have and not the pallid color it had been.

As was the custom, the Grabans insisted that Josh have coffee and a fresh roll before talking to Tommy. They all sat at the kitchen table with Tommy joining them and doing most of the talking.

"He's been talking constantly, Josh. I think he's making up for all those months of not saying anything," Betty joked.

"I brought along the videos for Tommy to see and let's hope he can pick out the attacker this time," Josh said and then looked at Odell for some encouragement that everything would be all right. Odell nodded, indicating to Josh not to worry.

When they had finished their rolls and coffee, Josh got up with the DVDs in hand.

"You won't have to do that, Mr. Trimble. I can tell you who it was who took my mommy and Shara and Janet away from me," Tommy said calmly.

"Who was it, Tommy?" Josh asked, curious and relieved.

"It was the man from the church, the man who gives the sermons."

"Pastor Bartholomew?"

"Yes, it was him. I could see him from under the bed. He came in the bedroom and turned on the light. He was looking around and then left. I could see his face in the mirror on the wall just before he turned the light back off. I remember he was doing a lot of talking and he was using bad words. I remembered his voice from the church."

"Any thing else you remember, Tommy?"

"Not really, I was sleeping and I was woke up by his loud talking. I got scared and crawled under the bed and that is when Squeaky came in and cuddled by me. I didn't see anything else but after I heard him leave, I crawled out from under my bed and looked for my mommy and my sisters. I seen them all bloody and that's all I remember," Tommy said. Josh noticed that his eyes were starting to get red and he watched a couple of tears trickle down each side of Tommy's face.

"Thanks, Tommy. That's all I need for now. You have been a big help."

Josh had plenty to do. He excused himself from the table and thanked the Grabans for the rolls and coffee. He also thanked them for all they had done and for their help.

Josh left the Graban house and drove directly to the county attorney's office to meet with Jim Bowden. He told him of his conversation with Tommy and requested a search warrant of the pastor's rectory, the church, and his residence. With the information that Bowden had so far and with the identification of Bartholomew, he agreed to draw up the warrant immediately and get it signed by a Judge. There would be plenty of probable cause to present to the Judge. The County Attorney felt there would be no problem with the Judge signing the warrant. Two hours later, the warrants were prepared, signed by the Judge, and issued for Josh to serve.

Josh brought the warrants to the Sheriff's office where the Sheriff, Frank Blume, and Deputy Jenks were waiting for him to arrive. They decided to serve the warrants simultaneously. Josh and Deputy Jenks would search the rectory and the church while the Sheriff and Deputy Blume would search the residence of Pastor Bartholomew. The pastor's house was next to the church so they would be able to be in constant touch with each other.

Amy Van Pre was sitting at her desk typing the church bulletin when Josh approached her. "Is the pastor in?"

"No, I haven't seen him all day. Can I help you?"

"Amy," Josh said in a serious tone, indicating to Amy Van Pre that this wasn't a social call, "we have a search warrant here for the pastor's office and the church. I would like to serve it on him, but as long as he is not here, I am going to serve it on you."

"How did you find out about the money already?"

"What money?" Deputy Jenks asked, confused by her answer.

"The money that he embezzled out of the church bank account. We only found out about it this morning when the bank called. Pastor Bartholomew took out over $300,000 in the last six months. A little bit at a time, but that's a lot of money and now the account is overdrawn. That's why you're here, isn't it? The bank called you, didn't they?" Amy questioned, nervously studying Josh for an answer. She reached for her purse, fidgeted for a cigarette, lit it, and inhaled as much as she could on her first drag.

"You say he hasn't been here all day?" Josh asked.

"No, and that's unusual. He's always here on Monday mornings. It's one of the busiest days. But I guess if he's got our $300,000, he's long gone by now," she stated, taking another long puff on her cigarette. "Did you know about the burglaries?"

"No," Josh lied. "Tell me about them."

"We've had three burglaries here. I mean whoever did them tore the pastor's office apart. They made a real mess and then I had to clean up everything. It would take me the whole day just to clean and put everything back in its place. I wanted to report them but the pastor wouldn't let me. But you know something funny. I told the pastor about it too but he didn't seem too concerned. The burglaries always happened after there had been one of those murders. I should've come to you right away, but I listened to the pastor. I mean he was my boss and everything. If I had it to do over again, I would have."

"Was anything taken?" Josh asked.

"I guess not. I always asked the pastor and he said that nothing was missing. Doesn't that seem kind of funny to you?"

"It sure does. Will you do me a favor? When you get a chance, will you go down to the Sheriff's office and make out a report on those burglaries? We'll need that information," Josh asked, knowing that this information would help back up Diaz's story.

Josh turned to Jenks and asked him to get on the radio with the Sheriff. "Tell the Sheriff that Bartholomew is not here. If he isn't at his house either, have the Sheriff tell his men to be on the look out for the pastor. If they see him, arrest him."

Josh began searching the rectory while Tom searched the church area. When Josh was done with the office, he joined Tom in finishing the search of the church. Nothing was found in the church or the office. Apparently, the pastor had gotten nervous because of the burglaries. If there was any evidence, it was either destroyed or put someplace else.

Josh grabbed Tom's hand held portable radio and called the Sheriff to inform him that they had finished searching the church and had found nothing. "How are you guys doing over there?"

"I think we might have found something. Why don't you and Tom come over here and look at it."

When Josh and Tom arrived at the pastor's house, they noticed the Sheriff and Frank were standing at the dining room table looking at an open bible that was in front of them. "You guys come over here," the Sheriff said. "Look at the inside of this bible."

The inside of the bible had been carved out and inside was jewelry, a lot of jewelry. There were rings, necklaces, earrings, stick pins, and bracelets. The Sheriff pulled out a gold necklace with a gold cross attached to it holding up the necklace with his pencil. "This might be the necklace that the Diaz girl was wearing and the one that Mr. Diaz has been looking for. I'll bet each one of these pieces of jewelry is from a murder."

"It looks like it. The captain probably gave them to the pastor as a present or something. The necklace does look like the one described by Diaz," Josh said looking at one more piece of evidence that was going to help convict Bartholomew.

The Sheriff pulled out the portable radio from the leather case attached to his belt; he was being called by one of his deputies. "Go ahead, Bones."

"I was thinking about your radio message earlier and I remember seeing the suspect in his car heading for Cedarton a little over an hour ago. He was in his uniform and he looked like he was in a real hurry."

"Thanks, Bones. Contact the Cedarton PD, let them know what we have and have them be on the lookout for him. I want you to head up to Cedarton and see if you can locate his vehicle. We'll head that way too."

Deputy Blume and Deputy Jenks drove back to the Sheriff's office with the evidence they had collected at the pastor's house. They had to classify it, label it, and store it in their evidence locker immediately so as not to break the chain of evidence. The Sheriff and Josh started toward Cedarton. When they were four miles away, Bones radioed again. "I've spotted the suspect's car at the airport. I'll meet you there."

The Sheriff's car pulled into the airport where they spotted Bones and drove up to where he was parked. Next to Bones' squad car was the pastor's car.

"While I was waiting for you, I noticed the tires on this car and it looks like the tread might match the tracks left at the Blake murder."

"I'm sure they will," Josh answered. "Let's go inside and find out where he went."

The three entered the small airport office and found a woman sitting at a desk reading a Michael Crichton novel. She looked up, smiled, and said, "Hi Sheriff, what are you doing here?"

"Are you the one that a pilot would check in with before he took off?"

"Yep, everyone stops in here and files their flight plan with me and gets the weather report."

"Do you know Captain Bartholomew?"

"Yes, in fact he was in here this morning."

"Where was he going?" Josh asked.

"Sioux Falls. He's the only one that flew out of here this morning."

"Did he say anything else to you, anything unusual maybe?" Josh asked again.

"Nothing. He just filed his flight plan and checked on the weather. The only thing he asked was if the weather was as nice up north as it was here. He said he was thinking about going fishing up north when he got back. I told him it had been beautiful all over the State today. That's all that was said."

"What time did he leave?" the Sheriff asked.

"Let's see," she said as she glanced at her last entry in the flight log. "He left three hours and ten minutes ago. He should be in Sioux Falls in about an hour or less. He's got a slight tail wind so he may arrive a little earlier. It's a four and a half hour flight but he should be able to do it in under four hours."

"Can I use your phone?" the Sheriff asked and was given permission. He called his office and asked to talk to Frank. He told the Chief Deputy what they had found out and had him contact the airport in Sioux Falls and also contact the authorities there and have them go to the airport in Sioux Falls and arrest Bartholomew on suspicion of murder.

"Thanks," Josh said to the woman behind the desk. "If you hear any air traffic from the Captain, would you call our office immediately and let Deputy Frank Blume know?"

"Sure will," she said and went back to reading her novel.

At the same time the judge had been signing the search warrants, Captain Bartholomew was pulling onto the tarmac with the Army's olive green, single engine Cessna preparing for take off. Captain Bartholomew, the pilot, the survivalist, and the paratrooper, was studying his flight plan to Voyageurs National Park in northern Minnesota. The last known contact with his plane came into the airport at Brainerd. It had been recorded and the transmission had been short. All that could be made out was "I'm going down, no fuel, no place to land."

The following day, the Cedarton Chronicle carried as its lead front-page story

"LOCAL PASTOR PRESUMED DEAD IN PLANE CRASH".

36333092R00136

Made in the USA
Middletown, DE
30 October 2016